THE SCANDALOUS SPINSTER

The Spinster Society
Book 1

By Alyxandra Harvey

ARE YOU SIGNED UP FOR DRAGONBLADE'S BLOG?

You'll get the latest news and information on exclusive giveaways, exclusive excerpts, coming releases, sales, free books, cover reveals and more.

Check out our complete list of authors, too!

No spam, no junk. That's a promise!

Sign Up Here

www.dragonbladepublishing.com

Dearest Reader;

Thank you for your support of a small press. At Dragonblade Publishing, we strive to bring you the highest quality Historical Romance from some of the best authors in the business. Without your support, there is no 'us', so we sincerely hope you adore these stories and find some new favorite authors along the way.

Happy Reading!

CEO, Dragonblade Publishing

Additional Dragonblade books by Author Alyxandra Harvey

The Spinster Society Series
The Scandalous Spinster (Book 1)

The Dainty Devils Series
The Duchess Games (Book 1)
The Countess Caper (Book 2)
The Husband Heist (Book 3)

The Cinderella Society Series
How to Marry an Earl (Book 1)
How to Marry a Duke (Book 2)
How to Marry a Viscount (Book 3)

CHAPTER ONE

London, 1816

L ADY CLARA PRESCOTT was invisible.

It was useful if a little demoralizing.

She could walk into a ballroom and half a dozen people looked right through her. As a debutante, it had been devastating.

As a spinster, it was expected.

After all, what good was a knife if you saw it coming? A sword might cut your head clean off, but it was also showy and dramatic. Two things that Clara had never been accused of in all of her twenty-nine years. A kitchen knife was...subtle. Unexpected.

Though the Spinster Society had plenty of swords at its disposal, it generally preferred kitchen knives. What better to defend the ladies of Mayfair, debutante to wealthy widow, than the unassuming, overlooked kitchen knife?

As such, Clara cut through the glittering crowd gathered to dance and flirt and fill the long, empty evenings. Not that different from their days, actually. She had arrived at the townhouse in Grosvenor Square, dressed in a gown that neither flashed nor drew notice with its obvious outdatedness. It was simple, modest. Bordering on prim.

Dull.

Like all of her dresses.

But it rendered her invisible, which was the point and had been the point long before she joined the Spinster Society. Tonight, it saw her through the door with barely a glance from the master of ceremonies and not a flicker of recognition from their host, whom she had met the day before.

Again, both useful and demoralizing.

She circled the room once but did not take a dance card. She never did.

Instead, she made her way upstairs. The ladies' retiring room at these fancy balls was her battlefield. Whispers, warnings. Consequences.

The Spinster Society dealt in consequences.

Clara slipped into the retiring room while most of the other guests were occupied at supper. It was a large parlor modified for the use of ladies, furnished with looking glasses, baskets of sewing supplies for gown mishaps, smelling salts. And, in the houses run by ladies of a certain mettle: whiskey, wine, and snuff.

The common denominators in every house and at every event were privacy screens hiding a row of chamber pots. It was customary for the Spinsters to leave warnings of cruel or degenerate men looking for wives in such places. Others had begun to add their own notices until some privacy screens were as papered as Covent Garden. There, placard men advertised lilac soaps and brooms and bonnet boxes. Behind the ladies' retiring room screen, information of a certain kind was distributed instead. Vital information usually kept from women.

Such as lists of gentlemen who did not mean them well and the women who helped them.

Clara ducked behind the screen and pulled the rolled parchment from her reticule. A new list of names to add to the poster someone else had already put up before she arrived. Lady Priya Langdon, who had founded the Society, would be well pleased.

The men in question would not.

It was dangerous business, being a Spinster.

For the others. Clara's invisibility suited her for the delivering of messages, the taking of notes.

Pity.

She emerged from the screens just as two ladies entered the retiring room, laughing together. They glanced at Clara, nodded.

"See, didn't I tell you there would be notices here?" one of them said when she stepped behind the screens.

"Anyone new?" her friend asked. She lowered her voice. "There wasn't much when I came in earlier. Do you think she's the one who put them up?"

"Lady Clara Prescott?" was the reply, all derision and disdain. "I hardly think so. I once heard her publicly correct the Dowager Duchess of Whitby's grammar. It did not go well."

"I imagine not."

Clara remembered that afternoon perfectly well.

One did not easily forget humiliation, even if it was wielded on purpose by her very self. She had needed the camouflage. She had secrets worth keeping, worth any manner of embarrassment. Misdirection.

It was very effective.

Also, the Dowager Duchess of Whitby's grammar was atrocious.

She slipped out into the hall just in time to see Miss Sybil Taunton, the most reckless of the Spinsters, sprint off. She was grinning, her gown dripping with green glass beads. She did not greet Clara, barely glanced at her, but she handed her a letter as she dashed past. Clara immediately dropped it into her reticule. The evening's mission was a success, despite evidence to the contrary.

Such as the two footmen giving chase.

Clara was fairly certain one of them was armed. It would give an ordinary person pause. It only made Sybil laugh. "Goodnight, boys," she called out, leaping onto the banister as though she was riding sidesaddle and sliding all the way down to the ground, and then promptly out a side door into the darkness of the gardens.

The footman thundered after her, swearing. The oil lamps rattled on the tables. The one with the dagger outline under his coat glowered at Clara. "Did she talk to you?"

Clara pressed herself to the wall, like any self-respecting wall-flower. "I beg your pardon?" she said primly.

"Never mind her," the other footman snapped, halfway down the stairs.

No one ever did.

But when they returned moments later with a shout of "Oi, check that pale little thing just in case," Clara felt very much noticed.

With the letter burning like a beacon in her reticule, she had two options: fight them if they tried to search her or run.

She chose to run.

⇒⇒⇒⫸⫷⇐⇐⇐

SYBIL MADE IT look easy. Clara did not. And she did not *feel* at ease, currently clinging to the second-story wall by her fingertips, the toes of her slippers wedged into a trellis.

At least it wasn't raining.

The sky gave a considering grumble. She glared at the heavy yellow London clouds. "Don't you dare."

Rain or not, she could do this. It was her first foray into the field, however accidental. She would not go home unsuccessful.

Running had seemed like a good idea, when she assumed she had a place to run *to*. Hiding was her next best option. There was another footman stationed deeper into the house, but she had slipped right past him, being invisible. The lady who had snuck into the upstairs parlor with the host's son was not. She was stunning—glossy hair, gleaming smile, glittering diamonds.

Luckily, she and the son were locked on to each other when they barged in unannounced.

And so out the window Clara went.

This sort of work was not generally under her purview. But she very much wanted it to be. She did her part, but she wanted her part to be *this*. Exciting. Daring.

Although possibly with both her feet firmly planted on the ground.

She probably wouldn't break any bones if she fell. But she might alert someone, which was so much worse. The problem was, Clara was a tiny bit stuck. She was grateful for the stones jutting out unevenly and for the trellis, but she had not had time to get a proper look at her escape. Was it strong enough to hold her completely? Should she go right or left? The side gardens were full of shadows, with no helpful torchlight to guide her. Even the moon was tucked away behind those threatening clouds.

And her fingers were starting to go numb. It was rather a cold February night to be dangling.

Bollocks.

She couldn't go back up—no telling where the host's son's tongue was now. Down it was.

Somehow.

Eventually.

"What the devil are you doing?"

Bram.

Of course, Bram.

Captain Bram Thorn. Tall, imposing, practically seething with authority and strength. *He* would never get himself caught hanging out of a window.

In a plain, unbecoming dress, no less.

She squeezed her eyes shut briefly, then straightened her spine. Metaphorically. Her spine was quite busy at the moment. Holding her up. Mostly.

She would sprout wings before asking him for help.

Bad enough that he was often there when the *ton* looked through her, or worse, rolled their eyes behind their fans at her approach. She was used to it. It did not mean she wished for Bram of all people to think of her the same way. Small. Plain. Easily overlooked.

Which was ridiculous. Bram didn't think of her at all. Why would he? He was a decorated navy man.

None of which was particularly helpful at the moment.

Especially as he was meant to be waiting at the carriage. He took her to and from balls and soirees with hardly a word. And now, the one time he had to leave his post to find her, he found her clinging to the bricks like a tree frog.

Perfect.

"Clara, listen to me carefully. Move your left foot outward. Bit more."

He guided her with that rough, gravelly voice she loved too much. With his ridiculous muscles and his scars and the crease at the corner of his blue eyes from staring into the sun and wind on a battleship, he was distracting at the best of times.

This was not the best of times.

Tell that to the instinctive unfurling of warmth in her belly. At least she wouldn't freeze to death before plummeting to her death.

"You're not going to die," he said sharply. "Pay attention."

She always paid attention. It was the cornerstone of her reputation: too much paying attention to rules and etiquette and *shoulds* and *should nots*.

Her fingers started to cramp.

"You're almost there. When I give you the word, you let go."

She laughed once, incredulously. "Bollocks to that, Bram Thorn."

A short silence below her. She wasn't supposed to say things like that. There were a lot of things she wasn't supposed to do.

"Clara." There was a thread of warning in the way he said her name, when usually he said very little and only very calmly.

"Captain Thorn," she returned through her teeth.

"I've climbed up on the stone railing. I can almost reach you. It's not as far as you think."

"I'm not jumping!"

"I'll catch you."

Why did that promise turn the warmth to outright heat that threatened to linger in her bones and blood for days, weeks, to come?

"*Now*, Clara."

It was the order of a man used to ordering other men to kill or be killed, to face a storm head-on, to take on Napoleon's army and pirates alike.

Clara let go.

She barely had time to register that she was falling when she landed in a pair of strong, muscled arms. When she finally opened her eyes, he was so much closer than he had ever been before. There was something in his pale eyes—affection? Pride? For her? Surely not.

"Good girl. Can you stand?"

Of course she could. But why would she want to when he was so warm and solid and smelled of sweet limes and salt? Like the sea, as if it clung to him and would not let go.

Because she was Clara Prescott. Not the beautiful woman upstairs in the red dress, nor the ladies flirting over their fans just beyond the wall.

She cleared her throat. "Of course I can stand."

He frowned, briefly. The muted light from the window behind him caught in the silver in his hair, the way she wished her fingers could. He was so handsome in that gruff way, older than she was by at least a decade, perhaps more. No one crossed him, not even the polished gentlemen she was more accustomed to interacting with, however briefly.

He set her down, and she stepped back. "Thank you, sir."

He raised an eyebrow. "What exactly were you doing?"

She pulled the letter from inside her bodice where it did not quite fit, but she had worried she might drop her reticule while clambering out of a window like a woman with very little sense. She could have sworn his eyes tracked the movement hungrily.

More wishful thinking. She was letting her imagination run away with her again.

"Mission accomplished," she said.

"And the mission required reckless behavior?"

She had never been accused of being reckless before.

She rather liked it. A lot.

Too much.

Something else to think about later.

"A couple decided to make use of the parlor before I could exit in the more traditional manner," she replied drily.

"Did they—" Bram glanced up and cursed.

He turned her so swiftly, she barely had time to react. And then she was pressed to the iron railing, his body against her back, and all the wrong parts of her brain were reacting.

Fine, it was her *body* reacting. Her brain was not currently responding to commands. It was issuing them, and they were not appropriate. *Closer. More.*

"Stay still," Bram growled, his voice rumbling through her. He leaned his arms against the railing on either side of her, as if it was the most natural thing in the world. As if one tiny sway forward wouldn't have him pressing against her. Or, with one tiny sway backward, her against him.

"Blighter's at the window. Must have heard us, but he can't see you if you stay put." He was large enough to block her from view completely, even without his greatcoat. His stance was nonchalant, his voice anything but. It stroked down the back of her neck, where his breath ghosted against her skin. She'd read about these kinds of moments. Dreamed about them. Written about them.

They did not compare.

"Clara," he said sternly, quietly. "If you sigh like that again, I'm going to take it as a challenge." She hesitated. He groaned, barely audible. "Don't."

She shouldn't. More importantly, she couldn't. They were on a *mission*. And he likely felt sorry for her, amused at her reaction.

The lonely spinster. The wallflower. A sparrow among swans.

That put the starch back in her spine. She would not be pitied, not by him.

The window above them slammed shut. She did not relax. How could she? Every inch of her was tingling, and it took all of her concentration not to let it show.

"Thank you, Captain Thorn."

She felt his smile against her hair before he pushed back, stoic once more. "Lady Clara. Let's get you back."

He led her through a gate hidden behind a lilac bush and onto the street, clogged with waiting carriages. No one saw them emerge. He didn't say another word, not as he handed her up into carriage and not when he helped her down again at the Society's headquarters.

"Any trouble?" Priya asked from where she waited in the foyer. She wore her thick gardening apron over her dress even at this time of the night.

"You know Sybil," Clara murmured, handing her the letter. "Is she not back yet?"

"No, she—"

"Here I am," Sybil crowed, sailing through the front door, disheveled and thoroughly pleased with herself. There was mud on her neck and leaves in her hair. Her dress was utterly ruined. "That was fun."

"And you, Clara?" Priya asked. "Any trouble?"

Clara smiled. "Yes. Finally."

CHAPTER TWO

London, one month later

THE SPINSTER SOCIETY headquarters looked like any other house on a street that looked like any other street in Mayfair. Only those who knew what to look for saw it for what it brought. Sanctuary. Justice.

Revenge.

Though Clara could respect all of those things, she was not here for any of that. Today, she was here to pour tea.

She demonstrated the proper way to offer cream or honey or lemon, how to stir without striking the edge of the cup, how to put down a spoon without spattering the tablecloth. Important things. Useful things.

Dull things.

It was her own fault, really. One night clinging to the outside of a building would not change her entire life. This was who she had constructed herself to be: a painfully proper lady. This was how she was of use to the Spinster Society.

She might have snored if snoring were a thing ladies could do. Instead, she served another cup of strong black tea.

Priya smiled, her dark eyes shining. "Thank you, Clara." She turned her cup in its delicate saucer. Miss Cunningham watched with rapt attention, perched on the edge of a cushion embroidered with unicorns wielding bloody horns. Clara knew Meg Swift, now the Duchess of Thorncroft, was no doubt behind the needlework. Everyone she knew, however peripherally, was *interesting*.

"Did you catch that?" Priya asked after a moment.

Miss Cunningham frowned. She was their newest member—recruit, really. She was a white woman with delicate features and still young to be a spinster, but her dowry had been spent by a drunk aunt. Her options had declined to nothing when word got out. And it always got out.

Priya lifted her hand, gold bangles, a gift sent from her mother in India, tinkling prettily. "This ring only looks like a locket for a lover's keepsake. In reality, it flips open on this tiny hinge, based off Tudor poison rings."

Miss Cunningham stared at the identical ring Clara wore. All of the Spinsters had one. "I knew there was something about this ring," she said. "How does it open?"

"There is a little indentation, just there," Priya explained. "I loosened mine earlier and then tipped my hand to drop the herbs in the cup. In tea brewed strong enough, the taste is undetectable. The effects, however…"

Miss Cunningham leaned forward eagerly, bloodthirsty enough to be a proper member of the Society already. "What does it do?"

"It causes an affliction of the bowels. Quite quickly."

"Brilliant."

"And I added laudanum drops to the teapot," Clara added drily. Much less flashy but just as effective. Priya had not asked her to, but sometimes you had to take matters into your own hands.

Miss Cunningham put down her cup hastily. The rattle of porcelain shivered through the room. "I do not care for laudanum." She blinked. "Pardon me, but *you* did that?"

Clara nodded tightly, reminding herself that she should feel vindicated at the surprise, not resigned. And it definitely should not sting. She knew why she was here: for deportment and etiquette and every dry societal rule necessary to navigate Mayfair. Not for poisons and espionage and all of the real reasons Priya had created the Spinster Society.

Priya had originally purchased the house next to her own in order to take over yet another greenhouse. She then proceeded to open the house itself to help defend the ladies of the *ton* against fortune hunters, and lords with too many suspicious dead wives, and parents willing to sell their daughters to any gambler or drunken lout with a title.

Not everyone had a powerful duke for a godfather, the way Priya and Clara did. They were known as the Cinderellas, mostly because he did delight in trying to marry them off. It was Priya's ability to collect secrets the way beachgoers collected seashells that had brought them here to this house with the Gorgon door knocker and the bottles of wine and whiskey on the sideboard. No lemonade or weak ratafia for the Spinsters. They had seen too many battles on the ballroom floor and in drawing rooms and picnics along the Thames. They had earned a stronger, less *ladylike* drink.

Clara knew that the others thought her too acerbic, too proper, and far too concerned with deportment. Manners were her king.

The other Cinderellas were not like her. Persephone used the rules to render her unmarriageable so she could continue her antiquarian pursuits—that was, until Lord Northwyck married her anyway. Meg used them to help her duke transition from being a millhouse manager in the north of England to one of the most titled men of the peerage. Tamsin utterly disregarded them, excused by the privilege of both rank and beauty. And Priya used them as a tool, as she used everything.

Clara used them as a shield.

There were precious few afforded to her, and one used what was at hand. That was a lesson she had learned all too well. And no one would ever suspect the truth about her. They would never consider it possible that she might stray from rules and etiquette and the holy temple of good manners. She'd seen to it.

It was *not* enjoyable.

She was as bored of parroting proper behavior as anyone listening to her.

More. Definitely more bored. So very, very bored.

She had hoped her help with Sybil at the ball would have Priya offering her more missions that did not involve pasting papers to privacy screens or delivering messages.

Apparently not.

She was not a beauty like the others, passable perhaps, but not enough to catch the eye of an earl or even a viscount, not with her particular reputation. Those who would esteem her for it, ironically, she could not abide. Even her parents had not been particularly fond of her. Her father thought her far too rule bound, her mother not nearly enough. And then they died and she was left with small annuity.

And her reputation, of course.

Popular opinion had it that it was worth more than gold.

It was not.

And it did not put food on the table. Or friends in her parlor. Or adventures at her door.

"I would not have let you drink the laudanum," Clara assured the young Miss Cunningham. "It was only to show that if you act exactly as expected of a lady, no one will bother with anything else you do. They will not suspect you."

It was more useful than she could adequately explain. No one thought Lady Clara Prescott interested in amusement, but she had dreams and goals and interests like everyone else.

Well, maybe not like *everyone* else.

She had enjoyed climbing down a house in the middle of a glittering social event. Much more than the social event itself. She had promptly begun a series of exercises designed to strengthen her arms. The next time she dangled from the side of a house, she would be able to pull herself back up.

And she had also spent an extra quarter of an hour scrubbing ink stains off her fingers this morning. Just in case. Not that anyone paid attention to her. Or would guess what she did when no one was watching. Not in a thousand years.

That was useful too. If a bit wearying.

Never mind.

You couldn't have everything, and she had what she wanted most. Two things, if you counted the Spinster Society, and though it surprised her, she did. It helped fill a void in her life that had begun to ache like a bad tooth. But it was nudged to the side, a wallflower even among wallflowers.

"Miss Comfrey is waiting for you in the pool," Clara told Miss Cunningham. Punctuality, after all, was another one of those bothersome rules.

The pool was set under a glass dome, with pipes running below that heated the water to a comfortable degree. Too comfortable for Miss Peony Comfrey, who preferred the ocean and ponds in midwinter. She had been recruited for her remarkable athleticism. Running, scaling cliffs, swimming across the Thames—all were entertainment for her. She was small in stature but strong enough to kick in a door. As she loved to demonstrate for new members. One never knew what skills might be required of a Spinster.

"Thank you, Miss Cunningham," Priya said. "Don't let Peony swim you to death. She forgets that not all of us can breathe underwater."

Miss Cunningham bobbed a curtsy and fled, eyes wide.

"Oh dear," Priya sighed, annoyed. "Do you think we frightened her? I thought she was made of sterner stuff."

"If she survives two hours with Peony, I don't think you have to worry," Clara said.

"True enough."

The war with France might be over, but the battles raged on in the heart of Mayfair. There were far fewer men who had returned than had left to fight. Memorials were held in every church, black bombazine wrapped the door knockers to many a fine house, ladies wore black. But it had been a year now, and the usual objectives rose to the surface. Establishing alliances between families, saving estates, growing coffers. Ensuring the family line continued now that so many second and third sons had been plucked from the world.

In short, marriage. Between too few gentlemen and too many ladies.

It had already been a brutal business, but now it was downright vicious. Aristocratic ladies were not taught skills that lent themselves to work, even if women were welcomed to work in the first place. Debutantes were on the shelf if they had not secured a match by their second Season. Spinsters and wallflowers were pitied, ignored. Impoverished.

But it gave them power. And Priya was more than happy to use that power against those who thought themselves above consequences of any sort.

The only reason the *ton* had not taken Lady Priya Langdon out at the knees was that she knew too much. About everyone. And she hated bullies. There were rumors of a scandal when she was a debutante, when her parents were in India where her mother was born, and her brother, Persephone's husband, was on the Continent fighting the French. But it was only a rumor, nothing anyone could truly verify.

As the clock on the mantelpiece chimed, cheerful chaos burst through the door. Two other members crowded inside, Lady Emmeline and Lady Matilda. Lady Matilda was soaked through, water pooling on the gleaming black and white checkerboard marble under her feet. Her bare feet. She wrung more water from her thick, dark hair. "Did you know the Serpentine is wet?" she asked cheerfully.

Priya handed her a towel. There were wicker baskets in every room stocked with various supplies: towels, soap, tweezers, alcohol.

"Did you find them?" she asked, unfazed at the mess and the

mayhem.

"Of course I did," Matilda said. "That's one fortune hunter who will not be abducting a lady to a forced marriage at Gretna Green. He is currently in the Serpentine. With his carriage. His horses are eating grass at the other end of the park. *They* were lovely."

Clara kept an eye on the time, battling envy. She still had to stop at the bookshop before it closed. That was something. A lovely something, and worth focusing on instead of the unpleasant twinge of jealousy and self-pity.

She wanted to drop a fortune hunter into the Serpentine.

Pierce Gallagher followed, taking the chair unofficially reserved just for him. He smiled at Priya. She liked to say that she had stitched him up when he was stabbed on her front doorstep, and then he had simply never left. What was more, he had brought with him a friend from his navy days, Captain Bram Thorn, to shadow the ladies, as shadowing Priya was a full-time occupation, however much she protested the matter.

Bram slipped into the room as well, taking his usual spot against the wall. Clara's eyes found him without any instruction from her brain. His gaze touched her, slid away. She felt it in her toes. He was imposing, handsome in a rough, steady way. It was difficult not to stare at him even when Clara had made it a bit of a lesson *not* to do so. It was a good deal harder than learning embroidery, or French, or the hundreds of unspoken rules and expectations that governed Mayfair. With a bit of an iron fist, it had to be said.

If there was one thing Clara knew, it was rules.

She was the worst of clichés. A prim spinster sweet on a sailor who could surely have anyone without extending any effort whatsoever. He did not have a title, true, but he was a war hero, for goodness' sake.

"Where's the whiskey?" Lady Matilda demanded. Her wild mahogany curls were a cloud of chaos around her head. Though Spanish was her mother tongue, she spoke six other languages, excelling with the naughtier words.

Priya grinned. "I've a lovely pekoe tea right here."

Matilda snorted. "I know the pot painted with the daisies, Priya. I'm not drinking *that*."

They were among the first invited to join the Spinsters and knew all about Priya's slightly disconcerting poisoning hobby. Nothing fatal, of course.

That they knew of. Honestly, Clara would not put money on that assumption.

Lady Emmeline was stunning, with curves and lush hips and the ability to befriend anyone. She sat with a smile while Matilda poured whiskey into small green glasses that matched the silk wallpaper and handed one to her with a wink.

There were many reasons to be a spinster. Sometimes it had nothing at all to do with the Marriage Mart and everything to do with love. It was obvious in the way the two ladies smiled at each other and how close they sat together in this house, where they were safe.

Clara accepted a glass as well, taking a bracing sip. She preferred brandy, whatever the etiquette might have to say on ladies drinking spirits at any time, never mind before supper.

"Why do you look cross as a chicken at sea?" Matilda demanded. With seven languages under her belt, she tended to mix her metaphors, creating new ones that made no sense at all. She always waited for Clara to correct her. Clara never did. Here in this house, she wanted to be anyone but herself. Even if no one would let her.

Matilda was right, though—Priya's expression was sharp, simmering with banked fury.

Never a good sign.

Priya moved to take her seat behind her desk, unfolding a letter. Her mouth was tight.

"Sybil is missing."

CHAPTER THREE

SYBIL HAD BEEN sent into the field some weeks back, posing as a chaperone for the ward of the Marquis of Eastbourne. Lady Heloise was nineteen years old, with an inheritance and a dowry comprising several thousand acres in Northumberland.

Which was hers upon her marriage to anyone she chose for herself. Her mother, a widow, had been clever and suspicious before she died.

Rightfully so.

And so, the marquis had hired chaperone after chaperone to keep the girl sequestered. If she did not marry, he would not have to give up her land.

The marquis did not like to give up anything.

Heloise's godmother, a very kind woman with no connections up to the task whatsoever, had sent word to Priya when her visits were routinely postponed. Priya had dispatched Sybil to investigate. She was a scrapper, having survived both the rookeries of Seven Dials and the glittering ballrooms of Grosvenor Square. The marquis would be no match for her.

Or so they had thought.

"What do you mean she is missing?" Matilda demanded, setting her glass down with a sharp rattle. She glanced at Clara as though she expected to be reprimanded for her manners. As if such a thing mattered at the moment. To anyone.

Clara kept her expression stoic, polite. It was practically a supernatural power of hers by now.

"She has missed her last two check-ins," Priya replied. "I sent a letter to the housekeeper, but Miss Taunton has not been seen for at least a week. And then I got this." She lifted up a drawing of a black dove with a thistle.

A warning.

Emmeline sucked in a breath. It was one of their codes, used when something had gone wrong or, if with a thistle, when they had to go on the run. "So she is in hiding, then, not missing exactly. Or at least she had warning enough to send us that. That's better, isn't it?"

"Marginally," Priya allowed. "Lady Heloise is also missing."

Clara winced. Going on the run with the ward of a marquis would take some careful planning. And luck. He had men and money at his disposal, not to mention the law. Sybil had an unholy love of chaos.

The way that Pierce took Priya's hand, reassuring and encouraging, was not comforting to the rest of them. Priya did not need reassuring. She was like a general, sipping tea and growing orchids while villains fell at her feet, skewered before they even knew there was a battle.

"Eastbourne is having one of his infamous house parties."

Clara had heard of them, if only in shocked murmurs. Masks, secret identities, sexual restraints flung to the wayside. Everything Clara was expected to disdain.

Everything she could not help but be ravenously curious about.

Brothels and sex clubs were not unheard of—in fact, there were entire streets in London dedicated to them. But such a gathering in an ancestral seat, filled with aristocracy mingling with the *demimonde*—shocking.

"That's why Sybil went when she did," Priya continued. "It was the perfect time to investigate him. The house will be full, and he's bound to be distracted."

"Not to mention soused."

"And he does not want the girl married and out of his control. Some of his chaperones have had more in common with jailers, according to her godmother."

"That *connard*," Matilda added in French, followed by Latin. "*Sterculinum publicum!*"

"Dearest," Emmeline said. "Did you just call him a public toilet?"

"Too right I did."

"That is why I love you."

"That and the way I can—"

"*Ahem.*" Emmeline cut her off with a cough.

"There are rumors about him," Pierce added in his Irish lilt. "None of them good. It does not bode well for Lady Heloise to be trapped in that house, even without the party."

"Well, he's not cleverer than Sybil Taunton," Matilda declared with the ringing of a sword being drawn from its scabbard. "I can promise you that."

"Not to suggest that we are not also cunning as foxes," Emmeline put in.

"Cunning as a fox with two heads," Matilda insisted.

"But even *we* cannot force him to just let her go."

"We forced that viscount to reinstate the dowager viscountess's annuity."

Matilda had "accidentally" pushed him into a pond and held him under until he acquiesced. She did have a pattern.

"We need one of his secrets." Priya tapped her chin absently with the end of her quill.

"The fact that he is lecherous and unscrupulous is clearly not a secret," Matilda replied. "So do tell."

"I don't know," Priya admitted.

Matilda widened her eyes. "You don't?"

"*Yet.* I don't know everything about *everyone.*"

"Next you'll tell me fairies don't exist and quite break my heart."

"I'm sure you'll survive the shock."

It was the quick, easy way they bantered that Clara envied the most. It sent a twinge through her, not quite pain but too close to it.

She sat up straighter. Bram found her with his eyes again.

"It's not just a house party," Priya said. "It's now a Devil's Night."

A sharp and heavy silence thrummed.

"How did I not know this?" Matilda finally demanded. She knew every social event from the Thames to the Isle of Skye.

"I only found out an hour ago."

A Devil's Night was even more notorious than the marquis's house parties. It was hosted twice a year by Lord Birmingham, nicknamed Devil. He carried the bank for an exclusive gaming hell that lasted a single night, hosted by a different lord. Earls, marquises, and dukes only need apply. It had to be someone unlikely to be punished—Devil's Nights never ran entirely smoothly.

And this year, the task of hosting had landed on the Marquis of Eastbourne.

No wonder Sybil had run. It was one thing to take on a lord, another thing entirely to take on the worst of the lot all at once with no assistance.

This could be Clara's chance to prove herself. To refuse to be banished to the drawing room once again.

Priya smiled grimly. "I'd go myself, but I've been banned from Devil's Nights by the Devil himself," she added. "Ridiculous nickname."

"I threw soup on the marquis last month when I was trying to get into that locked closet in his townhouse." Matilda shrugged. "I don't think I'd be welcome."

"I'll go," Clara blurted out.

She may as well have stood up on the furniture in her under-garments and declared she wished to race otters over the Serpentine. It would have drawn less of a reaction. Or *more* of a reaction. At the moment, the others were frozen.

"You cannot be serious," Matilda finally said.

"Maddie," Emmeline said quietly.

Clara tried not to take it personally when everyone turned to eye her dubiously. *Very* dubiously. Well, Emmeline and Matilda were dubious—Priya only looked more thoughtful.

Clara refused to glance at Bram. She did not want to see amusement or skepticism. Bad enough that he was always there to witness her humiliations.

"You?" Matilda asked. Emmeline nudged her with her elbow. Matilda glanced at her, then back at Clara. "It's not an insult," she insisted. "Only it's not exactly your...milieu."

"It's not," Clara agreed. But some perverse part of her, the stubborn, rebellious part she kept chained up, insisted.

Loudly.

This was for her. She could do this. She could help Sybil. And Lady Heloise. And prove herself.

"You haven't even read the Nightingale," Emmeline pointed out. "You said her stories were too naughty. Devil's Night seems like jumping from the frying pan into the fire."

"Never mind the frying pan—it's like jumping from the tea table straight into the fire. While on fire. With fire," Matilda added.

Indeed, Clara hadn't read the popular, scandalous love stories sold privately to women from a select bookshop in London for one very good reason.

She had *written* them.

She was the Nightingale.

Matilda would fall right out of her chair if Clara admitted it. Which she did not.

The rules might be constrictive and hypocritical and unfair, but at least she knew how to use them to protect herself. No one else would. Especially were she to be revealed as the authoress. No one would believe it at first, which was part of her strategy. Construct herself a prison so tame she could run wild without anyone's noticing. She knew something about disappearing.

But it meant that even when she became a member of a society such as the Spinsters, she was still relegated to pouring tea. Even after scaling a wall.

Fine, after dropping into the arms of a very muscular captain below. Same thing, really.

She knew that eventually some salient detail would reveal her identity as the Nightingale, and then all the doors of Society would be irrevocably closed to her. Even by the very ladies who paid good money to read her stories and whispered about them over tea. Especially by them. Popularity turned to notoriety with very little warning. And the *ton* loved nothing if not a fall from grace.

They would tear her to pieces.

Her family, the new earl who was a cousin she had seen twice since her parents died many years ago, would let them. He might even lead the charge, if only to keep himself out of the mud.

And so here she was, being accused of being too prim for her own books.

In front of silent, watchful Bram.

Again.

"I'm not a beauty," she admitted. "But they won't turn me away for that. Even if it is Devil's Night." She'd never been to a regular gaming hell, never mind this one. Nor a risqué house party. But she'd written about them. She'd written about a great many things she had never done. Torrid, delicious, flexible things.

"Don't be silly," Matilda scoffed. "You're as pretty as anyone else. You're just…reserved."

In other words, dull.

Emmeline nudged Matilda, again who huffed a sigh and fell back against the cushions. "I'm sorry if I never thought Lady Clara Prescott, doyenne of proper behavior, the type to attend a notorious event hosted by a known degenerate. You needn't act as though I've maligned her mother."

But Clara knew she was perfect for this enterprise. Both because of what the world knew about her and what it did not.

"Why you?" Priya asked bluntly. She could sniff out secrets like a French pig with truffles. Not that Clara would ever make that comparison out loud. There was nothing porcine about Priya. No gluttony, no obvious excess. She was as reserved as Clara, only she wore it like diamonds.

"Because," Clara said, "no one would ever suspect me."

A beat of silence.

"That's true," Priya said.

It *was* true. Just not the *whole* truth.

"Then it's decided."

Bram slipped out the door without a word.

Matilda pointed at Clara with all of the roiling drama of Macbeth's witches making their pronouncements.

"You are *not* wearing that matron's cap to a Devil's Night."

CHAPTER FOUR

CLARA WAS FEELING more feelings that she had felt in a good month, maybe two. Perhaps all year.

Her life was about to change.

She was full of worry for her friend Sybil—and anticipation, nerves, determination. No one would ever guess it, of course, in her gray gown and navy-blue cloak and with her too-pale hair tied tightly back away from her face. Her calm, polite expression. She looked as unassuming as she always did. Inside, she was turning cartwheels, the way she had done in the park as a child before her mother scolded her for being unseemly.

Finally, she was well on her way to being *truly* unseemly.

She was worried for Sybil, of course. Something had obviously gone wrong, but then, these things always went wrong in one way or another. And Matilda was right—there was no one better suited to taking care of herself than Sybil. She was in danger, no question. But they still had time to get her out of it.

Unease flickered through Clara, a spill of ink on a pristine white tablecloth.

What if she weren't up to the task? There was no telling what the marquis would do to keep that much land and its profits. What if she failed Sybil? And Heloise?

She could not. *Would* not.

She hadn't offered flummery before just to get herself sent to the marquis's estate. She really was Sybil's best chance—both to find out where she had gone but also to complete her mission. She knew Priya had already sent some of her other spies out to help find the ladies, just in case Sybil really had made it out onto the road somewhere away from the estate.

The marquis would be Clara's main concern. He was not to be trifled with. But he *could* be taken down, and she meant to be the one to do it. She would use her spinster camouflage to do the work of a real Spinster. Finally.

And there would be no need to climb down the side of his house.

Probably.

Even that did not bother her. She had been strengthening her arms and had scored the soles of her dancing slippers for better grip. Just in case.

Anticipation—downright excitement—thrummed through her. She hadn't felt the like in such a long time. She loved writing her stories, loved the covert nature of it. Loved that she was part of the Spinster Society in any capacity. But something just for her? A challenge? An opportunity to step outside the rigid lines she had drawn around herself?

She needed it the way she needed air. She was suffocating in her own life.

No longer.

She had to fight an uncharacteristic grin as she entered the Golden Griffin Bookshop. It was the kind of grin usually reserved for a new story or one of the schemes she and the proprietor, a Miss Kitty Caldecott, employed to get her stories to her publishers and payment back to her. Kitty was one of the very few people who knew who the Nightingale truly was. Clara's publisher and solicitor were the only others.

Kitty kept her secret. After all, the proceeds from being the only purveyor of the Nightingale's work paid her rent. Not to mention that Clara herself would rather buy books than anything else: food, sweets, diamonds. Anything. A great deal of her profits went right back into Kitty's shop.

The Golden Griffin was not particularly large, but it had more charm than any other bookshop in London. The walls were painted a moody, loch-gray blue, accented with gold trim and gilded chandeliers. Gold griffins prowled over the ceiling.

They carried the usual: poetry by Byron, travelogues, historical treatises. But where they truly excelled was in their collection of novels, mostly written by ladies, and other works such as those by Mary Wollstonecraft. Not to mention the naughtier books. Every time a pinched, starchy lady of the *ton* decried the declining moral standards of the shop, Kitty added another griffin. Clara had helped her paint the last one at midnight by candlelight over the crumbs of lemon cake. It was one of her fondest memories.

She did not have many close friends—or any, truth be told. She kept herself too aloof for that, and even the other Cinderellas, whom she had met every summer at her godfather's house, were usually a small army of their own. Clara's mother would not let her climb trees as they did, or dig for treasures in the dirt, or steal the raspberry tarts her godfather provided with the exact purpose of being stolen.

But she had her books and her ink stains and a freckled, red-haired bookseller with a stash of gold paint under her desk.

And now, a mission.

Kitty raised an eyebrow as she poked her head out from behind a shelf. Her bright green dress made her hair glow. "You are positively grinning, Lady Clara. How shocking. Unseemly, one might say."

Clara paused, looked over her shoulder.

"Shop's empty," Kitty said cheerfully. "You can allow yourself a facial expression."

Clara grimaced.

"Not that one."

She laughed.

"Better. What brings you here? Your...special order isn't due until tomorrow. Everything is in order—I've already checked."

"I know," Clara said. Her latest chapbook was being released that very week. "But I won't be here, so I just wanted to make sure everything was set."

"You won't?" Kitty was surprised. "You're always here on publication day."

It would be a wrench. Clara loved to see readers asking in hushed tones for the new book and spiriting it away in reticules—and once, memorably, down the front of a dress when the reader's mother came in. For the same purpose. Watching them circle each other was thoroughly entertaining.

"I'll be away for a few weeks. I'll leave the direction with my solicitor, should it be required."

"I'm sure it will all be fine. We've done this a dozen times already."

Half an hour later, Clara had made a little pile of books to be purchased for her trip.

"*Notable Families of Hampshire?*" Kitty read from the spine. "*Card Games and Their Rules?* Not exactly your usual fare."

"I'm branching out."

"Mm-hmm."

"What?"

"Fine, keep your secrets."

By the time Kitty had wrapped the books and placed them carefully into a box with a ribbon handle, the quiet had given way to the murmurs of shoppers in the narrow aisles. And a thump at the window.

Kitty marched to the door and yanked it open. "*Oi!*"

A shocked gasp from behind her, three from the sidewalk.

"You peddle sin!" The thrower of the egg now splattered over her window shouted.

"And you peddle misery, you rotten old cabbage!"

The older man turned purple with affront.

"Get home before I tell Grandmother," Kitty added, slamming the door. "My grandfather," she shrugged at the questioning gaze of a customer.

"Never mind," she added to Clara. "I've just had a delivery of gold paint. I'm going to paint the next griffin right on the outside wall, where he will see it every time he walks by. I'm going to give him my grandfather's walrus mustache as well, just see if I don't."

Clara admired her fire. And her willingness to wield it, consequences be damned. "If I return from the country in time, I shall lend a hand."

"Oh, good. You're the only one who can get the angle of the wings right." Kitty's gaze tracked a woman hovering by the counter, pretending to admire a set of music sheets. She winked at Clara and turned away. "Good afternoon—how may I help you today?"

Clara could only make out the whispered "Nightingale" because she was very accustomed to straining to hear it. She lifted a hand in farewell and stepped back out into the bustle of the city.

Carriages rolled past, the steady rhythm of the horses' hooves nearly lost amid the general cacophony. Her father's carriage had had the family coat of arms on the door. It was painted teal and lavender with ornate gold trim and was nearly as flamboyant as her father. There were peacocks who were less flamboyant. And common house sparrows who were more decorative than her mother. Clara hadn't been inside that carriage in years, even before the new earl took possession of it. It was now a very tasteful gray with sage-green accents.

She now lived in a perfectly respectable townhouse that her mother would have found akin to a brothel and her father drab to the extreme. She loved every inch of it, paid for with the earnings of her "torrid chapbooks," as one gossip columnist referred to them. But a carriage was an exorbitant indulgence when most of her other expeditions were within walking distance or done by hired hackney. There was no arguing that the family carriage was far more comfortable and had smelled far better. The walls were painted silk, the cushions laundered weekly. There was always a warming brick to keep her toes from turning into icicles.

No longer. Just a hired hackney with smoke-stained curtains.

Today, she felt too uncharacteristically energetic to be cooped up. She would walk home. There was the usual chatter and cries of flower sellers and street sweepers. The smell was purely London: coal smoke, horses, damp, flowers struggling to find the sun. Clara wove between pedestrians and shoppers and footmen lugging piles of boxes behind their mistresses. A dog barked somewhere.

A young boy, no more than eleven, popped into her path. "Lady Clara?"

She stopped. "Do I know you?" She could not think how. A woman wearing a silk dress the color of tangerines clicked her tongue at him when he did not dart out of her way quickly enough. He just grinned, a gap in his side teeth.

"Here you go." He shoved a letter at Clara and promptly vanished into the crowd, weaving between carriages with a laugh at every curse thrown his way.

Clara tore open the letter, wondering if this was some new form of communication from her publisher. Or the Spinsters.

It most decidedly was not.

I know who you really are.

She stopped in her tracks.

Not again.

CHAPTER FIVE

C LARA WAS NOT about to let a little blackmail sour her mood.
She reminded herself of that fact several times between washing her face, making sure her trunks were securely locked, and trying on three different pelisses and then deciding they were all an unfortunate shade of mud brown, so what did it matter which she chose, really?

And as far as blackmail notes went, it was fairly vague. But it still felt threatening, try as she might to convince herself otherwise. Someone had described her accurately enough to a street urchin for him to deliver the note, or else pointed her out on the street. Had he been watching her? Was he watching her now?

All the more reason to go to the marquis's estate.

It was bad enough that the first note had been slipped under her front door. She shivered just to think about it, and then scowled because this shadowy villain did not deserve her attention.

Even if he very much had it.

She had gone through her very short list of suspects: her publisher, her solicitor, Kitty. All people who knew how very much she wished to keep it confidential. All people who had more to benefit from keeping her secret.

Her publisher and her solicitor had signed contracts, and Kitty was her friend. Who else, then? Someone at the print shop or a delivery boy who had made a happy accident? Someone else at the publisher, such as a bookkeeper?

The list was both far too short and far too long.

Clara considered hiring a Bow Street Runner, but if she could not solve her own mysteries and avenge herself, how could she convince Priya to keep investigating for the Society?

And technically, no threats had been made. No demands. She supposed those would come next. All the more reason to leave London. Several weeks at a country house party was never something she looked forward to, but it seemed downright providential at the moment. Marquis of Eastbourne notwith-standing.

Bolstered, she pulled on her gloves and tied on her bonnet even though she detested wearing the thing. The Nightingale wouldn't wear frippery that itched her scalp.

But Lady Clara would.

Crisp spring sunlight glittered off windowpanes and chimney stacks. Off a black iron lamppost and silvery water melted from the vanishing frost.

Off Bram, pushing away from said lamppost, where he had been leaning when she came down the front steps to the sidewalk.

She blinked at him in case he was a mirage conjured by a fevered mind. She thought of him entirely too often, and now she had summoned him from the ether. It probably did not bode well for her state of mind. Blackmail threat or no blackmail threat.

"What are you doing here?" she blurted out. "I'm sorry, that was rude of me. How do you do, Captain Thorn?"

"I like it when you're rude."

She highly doubted that but did not say anything else, not until he strode toward the carriage Priya had sent for her as if it were a perfectly normal thing for him to do.

"Are you coming?" he asked. "I did not take you for someone who was tardy."

She did not move. "Did Priya send you?"

"She did not."

She was flummoxed. "She didn't?"

"No."

"You don't have a message from the Spinsters?"

"No, should I have?"

"I honestly don't know."

"Are you getting in?"

"I honestly don't know that either."

A fleeting smile came and went, softening his stern features, but only for a moment. "Lady Clara, I cannot let you go to Eastbourne's alone."

"Priya *did* send you!"

"No, but she did predict that you would argue with me. But *I* felt certain a lady of such impeccable manners would not argue with me out on the street."

He was teasing her. Just a little. In a way that brought her in on the jest and did not make her bear the brunt of it. Still, she crossed her arms.

"I can handle a house party, even one of that nature. They'll barely notice me." A galling thing to admit to him, but true nonetheless.

"You are not going to that house alone," he repeated. He did not sound angry, did not raise his voice. He did not even sound impatient. Just certain, as certain as he would have been proclaiming the sun rose in the east and set in the west. Facts were facts.

He was so handsome—the rough stubble on his cheek, the sharpness in his gaze. The line of his jaw and his shoulders under his coat. He took up space quietly, unapologetically. With nothing to prove. She envied him that. He was confident.

And stubborn. She supposed she ought to have expected that from a military man.

"You're not going to let this go, are you?" she asked.

His gaze was steady, direct. "What do you think?"

She sighed and took his hand when he offered it. Letters were tattooed across his knuckles: *HOLD FAST*.

She spent an unhealthy amount of time thinking about those tattoos.

And there was no sense in turning away assistance, not if it helped Sybil. "Fine," she said. "But this is *my* mission."

"Aye, Captain."

His fingers were warm and strong under hers. She suddenly wished she was not wearing gloves. He was near enough to block out the sun and the passing of strangers.

It occurred to her that climbing into a carriage with a man—shortly after receiving a threatening note, no less—was probably a bad idea.

What could she say? Some bad ideas were better than others.

⟫⟪

THEY RODE IN silence for the better part of an hour, until even Clara could not stand the respectful, excruciatingly polite nothingness.

Not from a man who took up most of the seat opposite her and all of the air in the carriage. It was extremely difficult to keep pretending that he did not affect her, that she did not regularly sneak glances at the breadth of his chest and the thickness of his thighs, when he was *right there*. There was nowhere else to look. Reading in carriages made her queasy, as did admiring the scenery outside the rocking window.

Trying to distract herself only resulted in very detailed daydreams of what it would be like if he were to seize her in his arms and kiss her. Would he be gentle, licking into her mouth? Would he overwhelm all of her senses, demanding and skilled? Would he take his time? She would wager that he would, methodically taking her apart.

Ridiculous spinster daydreams, and not the right kind of

spinster for this particular moment. She should be going over strategies, questions to ask, whom to ask them of, interrogation techniques. All things she had very little to no experience with. *Not* making herself blush, the pink creeping down her chest. Another reason she wore fichus, even when her gowns were already depressingly modest without them. Splotches of red did not improve on her paleness.

Doubt crept in again. What if she could not do this? What if Sybil and Heloise were doomed because Clara really was better suited to posting flyers behind the necessity at fancy soirees?

"I've never seen someone tense every muscle in their entire body at once," Bram said. "If you blink wrong, you might crack down the middle."

"What if I can't do this?" she blurted out, and then instantly regretted it when Bram's sea-blue eyes found hers. "Never mind."

"You climbed out an upper-floor window without hesitation, didn't you?" he pointed out.

"I hesitated *a little*," she admitted. It was very high up, after all.

"I am glad to hear it. Only a fool wouldn't have."

"Sybil never hesitates."

"*Sybil* is in trouble," he pointed out. "And *you* are the one Priya sent to help her."

That made her feel marginally better. It sounded logical when he said it. If this mission required planning and reserve and patience, then perhaps she was the right woman for the job after all. Sometimes you needed a little mouse to climb through the cracks in the foundation that no one else saw. A pale ghost to float through the house.

"What do you know about the marquis?" Bram asked.

Clara took her journal out of her reticule. The cover was embossed in simple letters: *Four Diocese Sermons*. No one every asked her questions when she read it, or *The Mirror of Graces* or *The Rudiments of Genteel Behavior*. Or anything meant for a vicar.

In actuality, the pages inside were filled with notes for stories she was writing, questions about realistic positions, wicked slang she overheard when walking in London. Today, they also had lists detailing the marquis, his reputation and his estate, and everything she had been able to find out about Lady Heloise, which, admittedly, was not much.

"His father died seven years ago," Clara said, struggling not to sound like a governess and failing. "He is the eleventh Marquis of Eastbourne. His reputation predates his recent title, even when he used his father's courtesy titles he was a bit wild. Nothing terribly out of the ordinary, mind."

"For a knab."

"Knab?"

"A toff. Their rules are different, y'ken?"

"I'm a woman, Captain Thorn." Not to mention an author of licentious and lewd stories. "Of course I *ken* the rules are different."

She knew the rules. All of them.

Before she could get tangled in that depressing topic, she went back to her notes. "He's a gambler. Obsessed with horse racing and does not care for Beau Brummell."

"A blow, I am sure."

"He has six estates, four in England, one in Ireland, one in Scotland."

"Blighter." Bram's Scottish brogue was particularly thick.

"And three houses in London. At least as many mistresses."

Really, it was the biography of any profligate peer of the realm.

They soon stopped at an inn to change the horses. It was well frequented, busy and welcoming with smooth, butter-hued wooden benches and the tantalizing scent of beef pies. They were clearly accustomed to highborn travelers, immediately offering wine, warming bricks for the feet, and picnic hampers with cheese and bread and blackberry jelly. Bram ordered two, as well as a small beer for Clara.

She blinked down at the thick brown beer. She wasn't sure

she'd ever tried it before. Miss Vinegar drank ratafia and lukewarm lemonade until she wanted to scream. She had earned the nickname during her first Season, and it had, regrettably, stuck.

"You look peaked, lass."

She sighed. "I'm naturally pale."

He half smiled. "I only meant you've too many thoughts in your head and not enough food in your belly."

"I've never had beer before."

"Never?"

She shook her head.

"Have a wee sip." He passed her the glass, his *HOLD FAST* tattoos dark against his knuckles.

She tried it, licking her lip when the foam stuck to it. It was heavy and rich and somehow tangy. She took another mouthful.

"Like it?" he asked after clearing his throat.

"I do, actually. Thank you."

The innkeeper chuckled from the other side of the bar. "Never had beer—that's a fine lady for you. But you're starting with the best."

"Did you brew it yourself?" she asked.

"Me mam used to," the innkeeper said. She had bright green eyes, shrewd and cheerful. "She taught me a trick or two." She motioned to her son as Bram poked his head out the door to see if the horses were ready. "Bring out the hampers," she ordered the boy before turning back to Clara. "He's a big one," she said, following her gaze to Bram. "Handsome too, despite the scars and those odd markings."

"I like his scars. And his tattoos."

She winked. "We always do. So where are you off to, then? Gretna Green?"

"No," Clara choked out. Not that eloping with Bram did not sound like a very fine plan. "Eastbourne Hall."

The innkeeper's face changed, the good cheer fading. Her smile dropped entirely. "The marquis's house party, is it? A fair few of you are traveling down that way."

"I imagine so." Clara took another sip, wondering if she should say something else. The undercurrents were deep and dark. She did not know how to navigate them.

"Have a care," the innkeeper added, saving her the trouble. "That one's clearly watching out for you, but even so, girls go missing at Eastbourne Hall."

Clara set down her mug. "They do?" Had the innkeeper seen Sybil? Heloise? "Did you know any of them?"

The woman shook her head, refusing to say more. "Go home, your ladyship. It's not worth it."

Going home was not an option.

CHAPTER SIX

Eastbourne Hall looked like something carved out of sugar instead of a house where women went missing. The gatehouse was sculpted with wreaths and lions and every curlicue the physical space would allow. The laneway curved gracefully through an oak grove to bring the carriage to a stop in the shadow of the great manor house.

The white walls dripped with decorative ivy. There were several turrets, and rows of Tudor chimney stacks lined up like toy soldiers. The extensive gardens were shedding their winter dresses of frost and ice. Tulips and daffodils brightened the bare shrubbery. Silk garlands of roses draped from the windows. Even Clara, whose own father was an ostentatious spendthrift who had once had all of his waistcoat buttons replaced with diamonds, had never seen the like.

She immediately felt like a tiny gray mouse about to be batted by a sleek cat wearing a pearl collar.

They were shown to the very last available room, which was situated in the dower house. There was another lady staying there who had already joined the other guests, which the housekeeper informed Clara with a slight sniff that did not bode particularly well. She stared at Bram. "I'm sure I don't know where to put you, sir," Mrs. Meadows said. "You won't fit in the attic rooms, I can tell you that."

"*Captain* Bram Thorn will require a *guest* room," Clara said sharply, so there was no confusion on that score.

The housekeeper winced. "No offense meant, my lady. But we are out of rooms entirely. I believe even the village inn is full. Some guests are sleeping two towns away."

"I see," Clara said. She wondered now whom she shared the dower house with, given that no one else had taken up the opportunity. Or been offered it.

"I'll sleep on the settee." Bram nodded to the parlor and the chairs clustered around the fireplace.

Mrs. Meadows looked relieved but torn. She clicked her tongue. "A war hero on the settee."

He smiled. "It's better than many a hammock on a ship, I assure you." He glanced at Clara, adding in an undertone, "And I'm not leaving you here alone."

Mrs. Meadows was already fussing. "I'll make sure they bring bedding and only the best tea trays. Do you care for scones? And shortbread, I reckon."

"You're a woman after my own heart, Mrs. Meadows," Bram said.

Mrs. Meadows blushed. Clara knew exactly how she felt. The soft burr of his voice, the kind, steady eyes. They were all very effective, especially from such a great height.

"Mrs. Meadows," Clara said, perfectly willing to take advantage of Bram's effect on the older woman. It made for a nice change that she was not the one currently moon-eyed over him. It took a remarkable amount of discipline. She'd never seen him wield that particular smile. It sent small, soft tingles through her. "I wonder if you could tell me where Miss Taunton is?"

Mrs. Meadows frowned. "Lady Heloise's chaperone?"

"Yes, she is my cousin, you see," Clara lied. It was so simple, really. No one expected someone like her to tolerate the immorality of lying.

Ha.

"I promised my aunt I would look in on her."

"I'm afraid she is not here."

"Oh? That *is* disappointing. I do hope she is working hard. We have a family reputation, after all."

"The marquis sent her to the seaside with Lady Heloise. You know how these parties can get. Lady Heloise is very sheltered."

"I see. A commendable precaution, I am sure." Mrs. Meadows seemed to believe what she was saying, which made sense. While the staff always knew more than assumed, surely a household staff numbering in the dozens would not *all* be able or wiling to hide girls away. But *someone* knew *something*. Clara was sure of that, too.

"But if you're her cousin, Lady Clara, she left something for you."

Clara and Bram exchanged a glance. His expression did not change.

"Did she?" Clara asked. It might be her first time using the cousin excuse, but it was one the Spinsters often employed. Sybil had run, or been taken, but not before she had put some precautions in place.

Mrs. Meadows fiddled with the ring of keys on her chatelaine, pulling one loose. "Here you are."

Clara accepted the key, trying not to look puzzled. "Thank you."

"She said you would know what it was for."

"Of course." She had no idea. "Thank you again, Mrs. Meadows."

"I'll leave you to get settled. Will you require a lady's maid?"

"Yes, please," Clara said. "That would very helpful indeed."

Once Mrs. Meadows had left, Clara raised her eyebrows at Bram, who leaned silently against the wall papered with pink and green carnations. "Sybil and Heloise are at the seaside, are they?"

"No one will question that for some time, if at all."

Clara examined the key. It was not overly large, but old-fashioned and heavy.

"Any idea what that unlocks, Cousin Clara?"

"Not a single one," she replied.

Still, she was further ahead than she had been, and they had just arrived. She had a secret message. A key.

Perhaps she was a better detective than she had thought.

⟫⟪

SHE WAS NOT, it turned out, a better detective than she had thought.

She was, however, exactly as unlucky as expected.

She had managed to ascertain—with some degree of subtlety, she hoped—that Heloise and Sybil had had adjoining bedrooms in the family wing. It made sense, seeing as Sybil was pretending to be an eagle-eyed chaperone.

Clara crept down the hall when everyone was occupied with dinner. Even the household staff would be focused on bringing dishes to and from the kitchen, preparing the final touches for each course, and on hand should any guest need anything. And truthfully, the longer Clara could avoid the fighting pits of High Society, especially gathered around a dining table like trapped ferrets turning on each other, the better.

She almost felt bad about abandoning Bram in the field. But she'd seen her chance and taken it. Sybil's key was safely on a ribbon around her neck, and she was wearing a perfectly acceptable gown for dinner. It would be the work of a minute to see the bedrooms.

Heloise's chambers were soft and beautiful, like being inside a delicate rose. Everything was leaf green and petal pink, from the damask wallpaper to the embroidered footstool. The writing desk was a confectionary of white scrollwork and gold detail. There were vases of flowers, novels in a perfectly arranged stack, a basket of needlework. In other words, perfect for an heiress.

Too perfect.

Where was the untidy ribbons thrown in frustration when it

would not tie around a neckline or a hair twist? The pictures from La Bell Assemblée of favorite dresses or bonnets ripped out and tacked to the looking glasses? The books on fairytales or the migratory patterns of bluebirds? The naughty chapbooks hidden inside the urn of silk peonies? The *personality*? Anyone at all could have lived here, from guest to cherished family member.

Clara knew when a scene was being set.

Not to mention that the armoire was filled with dresses, the closet with hatboxes and trays of pristine white silk evening gloves. There were walking shoes, shawls, pelisses trimmed with silver tassels. Everything a young lady might need.

For a trip to the seaside, for instance.

If Heloise was away for the good of her reputation, as purported, why were her belongings still here? Especially boots and umbrellas and thick pelisses best suited for seaside travel in March?

This bedroom solidified the niggling feeling that something was not right. For one thing, it was scrupulously tidy. Sybil tended toward the disordered, bordering on anarchic. Even when undercover. She might have kept the desk clear and the window-sills tidy, but there would have been boxes stuffed with trinkets, hatpins, books. Packets of herbs supplied by Priya.

There was only the serene, pale yellow of the coverlet and the matching cushions on the window seat, the painted chest without a single novel or wayward glove.

If Sybil had indeed slept here, it had not been for long.

Or else she had been erased.

Apprehension made Clara's heart race, even though there was nothing *obviously* untoward. A primal kind of instinct lifted the hairs on her arms, especially when the innkeeper's warning echoed in her ears. *Girls go missing at Eastbourne Hall.*

It was starting to seem less and less likely that Sybil had managed to get away and was hiding somewhere.

There was a sound down the hallway. Clara's heart beat faster and her skin prickled. She slipped behind the door, holding her breath until she was sure there was no one coming in, no one watching her. When she finally left the room and the family wing to join the party for supper, her palms were damp.

Bram narrowed his eyes on her as she found her seat and offered their host her blandest, politest smile. The marquis smiled back, all negligent charm and arrogance.

GIRLS GO MISSING at Eastbourne Hall.

With a warning like that, she knew better than to follow the marquis.

She did it anyway.

Dinner gave way to cards and wine in the drawing room, as it so often did. Clara slipped out to the ladies' retiring room, as she also so often did. She hoped for a privacy screen papered with bon mots, gossip, tidbits of news such as she was used to posting. She did not find any and so tacked some up herself. The number of women passing through these halls in the next week would be staggering, especially on Devil's Night. Forewarned was forearmed.

She was headed back to the drawing room when she heard the marquis's voice, cultured and bored. The very epitome of elegant ennui. She stepped hastily back, hiding.

He paused and snapped to the footman at his side, "Don't let anyone down there."

Down where? Why? It was his house—he certainly had the right to decide which parts he kept private.

As long as they were not filled with missing women.

He knew what had happened to Sybil, whether or not he had a hand in it. All signs pointed to it. So when he continued down the hall, she had to follow him. There was simply no other choice. She kept far enough back, walking lightly. She had never drawn attention before, so there was no reason to think she would now. The marquis did not care for women like her.

Thank God for that.

He stopped around the corner, continuing the conversation in hushed, irritated tones.

"...from the guests."

It was difficult to make out what he was saying. She dared not get closer. She strained but could only hear a word or two.

They fell silent and turned around, heading back to the drawing room. They were already walking her way. There was nowhere to hide. Best to brazen it out. A lady on her way to or from the retiring room was common enough.

The marquis was with one of his footmen who did not act like footmen, but more like boxers waiting for something to fight. Their gazes collided, the marquis with his square jaw and patrician features, his customary blue-velvet coat, and Clara, ever unnoticed.

Usually.

She found she vastly preferred being unnoticed. There was something not quite right in his eyes. She could not explain it, but it made the back of her neck prickle unpleasantly.

"Lord Eastbourne," she said politely, and kept walking.

Every hair on her arms lifted in warning. She did not falter, did not look back, though she had never felt more exposed. She turned the corner and finally released her breath, safely out of view.

And then she was yanked backward into the shadows, a whiskey voice in her ear. "Don't make a sound."

CHAPTER SEVEN

*B*RAM.

Her body responded before her brain fully recognized him. He glowered down at her before tucking her into his side. He enveloped her completely in his heat, his scent of rain and sweet limes. She was so close she could see the stitching of his coat, a glimpse of skin behind his loosely knotted cravat, not at all fashionably starched and complicated. She found she vastly preferred it.

"Don't move," he ordered.

She leaned into him without conscious volition, so moving did not seem to be an option anyway. At least not moving *away*.

"On second thought," he muttered to himself before tugging her into the nearest room, a small parlor reserved mostly for the lady of the house, had there been one. His gaze roamed from ornate chairs to a crystal swan roughly the size of a real swan, to an armoire painted with lilies. He dragged Clara toward it, yanked it open, and lifted her inside. He closed the doors in her face before she could make a sound.

She saw him through the crack of light between the wooden doors. He dropped into one of those spindly chairs that she was surprised did not break under him. His pause made her think he was mildly surprised as well.

And then a footman burst in—the same one who had been

receiving an order from the marquis, the one who did not carry himself like a footman. He had doubled back. Looking for her? For something else? *Someone* else?

He looked disdainfully at Bram, who could not have stood out more, large and sun-worn, in the elegant room that suddenly looked like a dollhouse, fragile and inconsequential around him.

"What are you doing in here?" the footman demanded in a way that would have been utterly foreign to a proper footman addressing the guest of a marquis.

Bram regarded him calmly, stoically. Maybe not so stoically. Clara fancied she could read him a bit better now—the lift of his scarred eyebrow, the clench of his jaw. Even through the gap between the doors of an armoire she shared with a morning gown and a fox-fur stole who stared back at her accusingly. There might be a spider in that upper corner as well, but as it seemed larger than she liked, she ignored it. Her pulse hammered in her ears.

"Snuck away for a smoke, mate." Bram pulled a pipe from his coat pocket. His expression was hard, daring the footman to continue his rude questioning.

The footman did not meet his gaze, but he did look around the parlor. Clara held her breath. *Don't see me, don't see me.*

Bram's concern had rubbed off on her. And however would she explain her position? Not that a regular footman would have the audacity to demand answers from an earl's daughter. She had paid off her father's footmen when she was a girl so they would turn a blind eye when bringing in her many packages from the bookstore. Her favorite footman had never needed a bribe. The rest mostly ignored her if she did not require their immediate assistance.

Not this footman.

"Have one of the ladies come in here?" he asked.

Bram settled back in his chair like it was a throne. "Beg your pardon?"

"A lady? Ghostly hair? Dresses like my grandma?"

"Why?"

"Sorry?"

"Why are you looking for her? Doesn't seem quite right, does it?"

"A message was delivered to her."

"What's her name?"

The footman frowned. "What?"

"The lady's name? In case I see her."

"Um."

"You don't know it?" Bram pressed coldly. "How odd, if you're to deliver her a message."

The footman swallowed. "Sir." He bowed and hastened away.

Bram did not move from his chair, but his searing blue eyes met hers through the splinter of light through which she was spying. He shook his head almost imperceptibly. Clara's hand dropped to her side.

It was a full five minutes before he finally crossed the room toward her. She pushed the doors open before he could reach them. "Did you just put me in a cupboard?"

"Aye."

She stepped out. "How did you know he would come back?"

"This house reeks of danger. I'd rather sail into a hurricane." He gripped her chin lightly. "Be careful, Clara."

Girls go missing at Eastbourne Hall.

CHAPTER EIGHT

CLARA WAS FINALLY sneaking out at midnight, and she was wearing a nightdress, a shawl, and thick woolen socks in her slippers. She would have to walk through the garden to get to the main house, after all.

Another woman might have made it look alluring. Clara was quite sure she did not.

No matter. There was work to be done.

But as a tale of danger and sensuality, it left a little something to be desired. Were she writing it, she would make sure, for a start, that she was wearing something a little more flattering. The sheer peignoir that she had purchased in a fit of optimism was sensibly packed in her trunk. One did not creep about in cold, drafty hallways wearing lace at this time of the year.

As she crept through the dower house parlor, she told herself she absolutely was not going to peek at the padded bench by the fire to see if Bram slept in nightclothes or eschewed them altogether. She would give away her best inkwell to catch a glimpse of his naked chest. It would be muscular, dusted with hair. Perhaps a scar or two, given the scar on his cheek and the ones on his hands.

Just one peek. For security's sake. To make sure he was all right.

And possibly gather inspiration for her next book.

Clara Prescott, you have a problem.

Or she would have, had Bram been stretched out on the bench as he ought to be. There was a small cushion, a folded blanket.

No Bram.

Had he gone back to the house? He would have been welcomed in any number of beds, she was certain of that. And this was the occasion for it. She refused to be jealous, because jealousy was absurd. The disappointment, to which she also had no claim, snuck in and took her by surprise.

It was not the only thing that took her by surprise.

"And where are you off to in the middle of the night?"

Bram's voice wrapped around her throat like stroking fingers. Her skin prickled, caught between surprise and excitement of a different sort. He was at her back again, a large, solid presence who dwarfed her completely.

She bit her lip, drew it into her mouth slightly.

"Don't do that," he murmured in her ear.

She desperately wanted to ask him what he meant by that, but he was already stalking around to face her with that serious, watchful expression.

"Clara."

"Yes?"

"Where are you going?"

Oh, right. She was supposed to be skulking. Sneaking. Not *yearning*.

Mortifying.

"To the main house, of course," she replied. A little too breathlessly, but not embarrassingly so, all things considered.

His eyes narrowed. "Alone?"

"As you see."

"No."

She blinked. "I beg your pardon?"

"You don't sneak around that house alone."

She blinked again. "That is quite *literally* why I am here."

"You wake me."

"At three in the morning?"

"Anytime. Every time. Promise me."

She frowned. "I can't possibly make that sort of promise."

"Please."

"I promise to wake you." She paused. "Whenever possible."

"Damn it."

She smiled. She couldn't help herself.

"Amused, are you?" he asked quietly. "I knew you were trouble."

She smiled wider. With her whole entire soul. She had never been called trouble before, not in that soft, knowing tone with a hint of fondness and more than a hint of warning. It made her want to do reckless, inappropriate things. With him.

To him.

"We should go," she said, suddenly very, very awake.

"At your service, Captain."

Very awake.

THEY CREPT THROUGH the house, navigating by the moonlight streaming through the windows. Clara did not dare light a candle, even though she stumbled. Bram, naturally, moved as though he could see in the dark. Her eyes watered with the effort to sort out shadow from furniture, carpet edge from floorboard. She stumbled again. Bram steadied her with one big hand and not a single word. He nodded down the hall when she reminded herself not to lean into his touch like a woman who did not write "torrid and deviant tales" for a living.

She had once written about a couple and their valet doing things no valet was hired to do. A lot. In every room of their Mayfair townhouse. And once in the back garden. Twice in the carriage.

She ought to be composed. Nonchalant.

She was not.

Right. Back to the marquis's study.

And, of course, the door was locked.

"Bollocks."

"Such talk from the proper Lady Clara. What would the others say?"

She wrinkled her nose at him. "Nothing good, I assure you."

Something passed over his face. Cold, displeased. With her? She couldn't tell.

"Wait, the key!" She lifted it out of the neckline of her dress where she had tied it with a ribbon.

It did, of course, not fit the lock.

"I knew it wouldn't be that easy."

"Step aside," he ordered. She knew exactly how good a captain he had been just by her instinct to obey. His eyes flickered over her. She swallowed and stepped back. Something she was very much afraid was arousal tingled through her core. She pressed her thighs together. His gaze sharpened.

It seemed an effort for him to focus on the door.

She was embarrassing herself. He knew she was drawn to him—he *must* know. The lonely spinster, disdained by Society. The handsome older captain. He must draw women like bees to honey.

She lifted her chin, straightened her spine.

It did not help.

"Why do you that?" he murmured, not looking at her as he crouched in front of the doorknob, the wood carved with roses.

Was he asking why she looked at him like she wanted to devour him? Why she suddenly wanted to kneel as well, but for a very different purpose?

"Do what?" she croaked.

"Stand like a soldier at attention when you're nervous."

She swallowed a hysterical giggle. She was turning herself inside out, burning with want, and he had no idea. That was better than the alternative.

Wasn't it?

It probably never even occurred her that she even knew what lust was. She was as appealing a hardtack biscuit. *Miss Vinegar strikes again.*

"There's nothing wrong with good posture," she said.

And she'd mortified herself all over again. Her voice was too prim, her words ridiculous.

She was a *Spinster*, damn it. It was high time she acted like it.

She watched as he picked the lock with a long metal instrument and a turn of his wrist. "Will you teach me how to do that?"

"I'll teach you anything you want."

That blaze of lust again.

Damn it, Clara.

They stepped into the study, lush and exuding power. Leather-bound books lined the shelves. A portrait of the marquis in a heavy gilded frame hung over the mantlepiece. "That sword is ridiculous," Clara muttered. "Overcompensating."

Bram's lips twitched.

There were crystal decanters, a gold watch fob, pen nibs. In short, a perfectly ordinary study of a perfectly ordinary, if libidinous, marquis. Even the papers in his desk were ordinary: ledgers tallying household expenses, letters from Tattersall's about horse auctions, a request from an orphanage in London for funds. Ink pots, candles, snuffboxes.

They opted not to search his private chambers when the creaking of the floorboard and the giggling suggested the bedroom hallways to be as crowded as Covent Garden.

She was not going to be discouraged, she told herself as they snuck back outside. She had barely begun her search, after all.

She knew better than anyone that what you saw was not always what you got.

CHAPTER NINE

WHEN THE SUN emerged, the afternoon offered a host of new entertainment: horseback riding, walks to the nearby ruins, flirting by the river.

Clara chose the library. Not just because it would be empty.

Mostly empty.

Bram had been serious when he said she ought not to go anywhere alone. He stuck to her like a particularly devoted suitor. At least to anyone else's eyes. Anyone who had never met her before.

Really, as a ruse, it needed work.

Bram did not seem inclined to worry about what the others were thinking. His only concern was that she not be left on her own anywhere the marquis might happen along. As if the Marquis of Eastbourne even remembered her name, or gave her a second glance except to wonder when he had invited her. She was not the type to attract his attention. Hence her being here in the first place. She really should not have to explain this again.

The library did not offer any secret family histories or locks that fit her mysterious key. It offered a quiet Scotsman who kept glancing out of the window. A tea tray sent by the housekeeper. Several family Bibles with names inscribed. Two chapbooks written by the Nightingale tucked into a corner. Clara hid a smile.

The Wallflower and the Wastrel. Ravished by the Rakehell.

Some of her most risqué work. An article had even been written on how *The Wallflower and the Wastrel* was a symptom of the problems ruining decent society and causing women to faint in libraries across the country.

Clara had added a fainting woman in the next book, found on the floor of the library and revived by a brawny professor wearing spectacles. It was her best-selling book to date. Kitty had added four gold griffins to her bookshop walls and bought her sister a new parasol with the profits.

When Bram turned in her direction, Clara shoved the books back behind a huge, dusty dictionary of Latin phrases. Still, nothing worth noting on the marquis and nothing at all on Heloise or her connection to the family.

Clara was not inspiring great confidence as the new weapon in the Spinsters' arsenal.

Until…

By chance entirely, she reached for a large tome on the wild-flowers of Hampshire and a scrap of parchment fell out. The handwriting was precise, careful.

"What have you found?" Bram asked, angling his body so no one could see what she was doing should someone join them accidentally. It was unlikely, as this was not a house party that centered around books, but Bram was wary, aways on alert. It would have served him well as a captain, that quiet watchfulness, the certainty that he could handle anything that came his way.

"A letter," Clara said. *"Please help me,"* she read aloud, her throat going dry. *"I don't know when my father met the marquis and I don't know why he chose him as my guardian, but I want to go home. He says he will send me to France on a vacation to see the art there, but I do not believe him. There is something wrong in this house. From a* Miss Blanche Yarwood."

"Who is Miss Yarwood?" Bram asked.

"Who indeed."

Girls go missing at Eastbourne Hall.

BRAM WATCHED AS Clara's posture changed again. She was a fascinating mosaic of moods and secrets chasing across her body like it were a canvas. She reminded him of the sky over the sea, constantly shifting and changing. Or like the water below, flashing green, silver, black. You never quite knew what waited beneath the delicate surface. He couldn't help but watch her. She made being landlocked bearable.

He hated having her inside this house with hidden pleas for help hiding in the books and a marquis in a fine blue-velvet coat expecting everyone to bow and scrape before him. He wanted her far from here. But since that was not going to happen, he would have to make do with watching over her. No one else did, even in London. It made him clench his back teeth to the point of cracking.

Why were the bloody English such idjits?

She slipped the letter into the sleeve and moved to another shelf. "I should have thought of it earlier," she murmured. She read the spines, the sun touching her blonde hair and making it glow like moonlight.

"Done what?" he asked, his voice rougher than he liked. He had been at war for many long years, a captain accustomed to cannon fire, blood in the water, wounds festering, and was now being undone by a slip of a woman who had no idea the effect she had on him. Sometimes he caught her blushing when she looked at him, those pale cheeks touched with a light pink that traveled down her neck. He ached to chase it down the neckline of her plain dresses with his tongue.

He knew better than to want what he could not have. She was fine porcelain, and he was clay.

"Sometimes the Spinsters leave each other messages in the libraries of houses such as this one." She touched the gilt lettering, reading titles. "Something wholesome and utterly boring that no one is likely to want to read but would look perfectly ordinary in the hands of a spinster wallflower. They always bring a copy with them. I should have as well."

He was constantly impressed with these women who operated under the noses of aristo knabs who thought themselves smarter than everyone else, especially ladies of good birth. They might fear Priya, and rightfully so, but they never failed to overlook Clara or Emmeline. Even Peony when she was not swimming across lakes or riding horses better than the acrobats of Astley's Amphitheatre.

For instance, no one in their right mind would want to read a book titled *Manners and Morals of A Virtuous Woman, Part Three.*

Clara pulled it out with a tiny sound of victory that went straight to his cock. He wanted that little noise for himself. Wanted it as his reward for bringing her to pleasure over and over again until she forgot how to blush. Until she offered him one of her secrets, of her own accord. He knew better, but he could not help but crave it.

Behind the book, tucked against the bookcase, was another key. Clara grabbed for it, frowning.

"Mean anything to you?" Bram asked.

She shook her head. "I'm afraid not."

"Not a message after all?" he asked.

"It most likely is, I just don't know what it means. This or the other key."

"It's early days yet."

"I'm not sure ciphers are Sybil's strong suit," she said drily with that wry humor no one else seemed to catch. "Or mine."

She turned on her heel, key in hand, tracking every detail of the enormous library. Books, painted globes, arrowheads and musket balls found in the moat now filled with wildflowers and burrowing rabbits. Oil lamps, candle sconces, a bronze sculpture of Zeus, complete with thunderbolt.

"White dove," Clara murmured.

She pointed above the bookcase that had housed *A Virtuous*

Woman. A tiny white dove was on a scrap of watercolor paper set among a collection of curiosities, fossils, rare books, an astrolabe. It was small enough to go unnoticed but did not quite fit all the same.

"Sybil left that," she said, sounding surer of herself than she had since they'd arrived. It transformed her, from moonlight to crystal. Both equally beautiful. "There's something here." She frowned at the books, the decorations. The candlestick holder set into the wall just below the dove.

"You're right," he said. "In Scotland, between smuggling and avoiding the bloody English, we have plenty of hidden corridors."

He pulled the candleholder down.

There was a creak, a puff of dust, and then part of the bookcase opened up. It was just wide enough for a person to walk through into the darkness. A person like Clara.

Bram took hold of her elbow. "Anything could be down there."

"Sybil could be down there."

"Or the marquis. Several of his burly footmen. A family of angry rats." He handed her the candle from the holder. "You carry that; I'll carry the knife."

She lit the candle, and he was grateful she did not argue or tell him to shove his head in the loch like his sisters would have. And his grandmother. His mother. But they could shoot a pistol and punch like boxers. He had yet to see Clara so much as make a fist. He did not know if she could protect herself, but he did know that she would never have to so long as he had breath in his body.

"Ready?" he asked. She nodded impatiently, holding the candle high. It sent spears of light around him, into the passageway. It reeked of dust and damp, but also beeswax. They weren't the first to come through here with a candle. "Stay close to me."

The way was narrow, and he had to bend down slightly to fit. They came across several peepholes cut into the walls, allowing a person to spy on those at dinner, in the smaller parlor, the conservatory. It started to slope downward. The air was thicker with disuse. Scurrying sounded up ahead.

Where they stopped at a door.

A locked door.

The candle sputtered. It was colder here, an unmistakable draft sneaking around the thick wooden planks. When Clara shivered, he stepped closer, feeling like a giant towering over a fairy sprite. "This passageway could be hundreds of years old," she said. "But Sybil wanted us to know about it all the same."

Even though none of her keys fit the lock.

IT WAS THE kind of social event Clara dreaded.

She would much rather be clinging to the side of the building again. Or sneaking through a dark, dusty passageway.

A drawing room blooming with aristocratic ladies whispering to each other and aristocratic men looking down their noses, all so glittering and beautiful?

Hell. "Beg your pardon?" Bram asked quietly when she came up short in the doorway. He wore black, his cravat in a simple knot, not an ounce of flash to him, and still outshone every man here. Most of them knew it, too, if their narrow-eyed glances were anything to go by.

"This is another circle of hell," she muttered. "Dante had no idea."

Bram chuckled softly. She felt it caress the back of her neck, felt it steal her breath.

This was getting ridiculous. A *chuckle* should not affect her, no matter how soft.

Bram only leaned back against the wall as if ladies fluttered every time he spoke, which they probably did. It wasn't even the bored, languid affectation of a lord with too much time and not enough occupation. It was the patience of the captain of a ship, waiting on the wind to turn. Prepared. Confident.

If she were another woman altogether, she'd lick her lips. Look up at him through her lashes.

Tear off his cravat with her teeth.

But alas, Lady Clara was in attendance, not the Nightingale.

Indeed, one of her heroines would have purred at him, her bosom a great deal more bosomy than Clara's would ever be. She would have said something witty, charming. Definitely wicked. Clara only blurted, more panicked than seductive, when the drawing room loomed before her, "Aren't you coming with me?"

"I'm here for you, not them. So I'm better served where I can see everything."

The man was starting to make her feel as though she had found herself in one of her own stories.

And she did not have time for it. No matter how she longed for even the pretense of it. He wasn't flirting with her—she knew it was her own fancy.

"Is that Lady Clara?" someone whispered. Loudly. Why bother whispering at all if you were going to turn it into a shout?

"Surely not, at *this* event?"

"And in that dress? She did not even bother to dampen it."

As if Clara was daft enough to wet down her dress in *March*. Catching a chill was not attractive.

Or was it? As always, places like this and guests such as these made her doubt herself.

"Dampen her dress?" One of the gentlemen snickered. "The only thing Lady Clara ever dampens is the mood. I can't think why she's *here*."

Clara stiffened but said nothing. There was no point. They weren't, strictly speaking, *wrong*.

Bram frowned.

It wasn't the comment that mortified her—it was that he was right there to hear it. To see her dishwater-pale hair and her boring dress and be forced to agree with them. She was no siren to lure men from their duties. Her nickname by the end of her first Season was Miss Vinegar for a reason.

Nightingale, she reminded herself, keeping her expression bland as milk pudding. *You are the Nightingale now.*

"Perhaps the marquis was in need of a naughty governess," Lord Howell suggested.

"*Her?*" Lord Faltingham laughed so hard that he spilled his champagne down his front.

Bram straightened away from the wall. Lord Faltingham glanced his way and then suddenly found himself fascinated with the spill on his coat.

Clara walked by as if she had not heard them. She didn't float gracefully or mince her steps. She wouldn't know how to. Her goal was to reach the settee by the window. They would stop paying attention to her by the time she sat down, and she was situated well enough to overhear a good portion of the conversations frothing through the drawing room. She did not expect to hear anything particularly useful about the marquis, but she had to start somewhere.

For one, he had just received a note from a footman. He plucked it from the gold tray, read it with a slight frown, and then took his leave. Abruptly. He made the usual apologies and kissed the hand of the lady on his left who wore red lip stain that made her look positively decadent.

And then he was gone.

Interesting.

Possibly. Perhaps his horse had just foaled and there was nothing more to it than that.

That would make for a horrible start to Clara's undercover career. Not dramatic at all. Priya had once locked the prince himself in a privy.

But as tempting as it was to follow him again, Clara stayed where she was. If she gave herself away, being invisible would not help her. More importantly, it would not help Sybil and Heloise.

The lady with the red lips and the dark hair curling over one shoulder approached her. The others watched, hungrily. Eager for entertainment. "May I join you?" the woman asked. "My name is Selene."

Clara had heard of her. She was a Bird of Paradise, the madam of a house called the Temple. She and her ladies were all named after the moon and stars because they allegedly only came out at night. And here she was, more welcome in a marquis's house than Clara was as an earl's daughter.

"Of course you may," Clara said, as someone giggled nearby.

Selene sat next to her with her a wry smile. "Pay them no mind. I expect it's a jab at me."

Clara snorted—she couldn't help herself. Selene might be scandalous, but she was also stunning and clearly very clever to be invited to the drawing room of a marquis. With a multitude of ladies present.

Ladies like Clara.

"It's a jab at *me*."

And though someone as devoted to the proper way of things would certainly be expected to look askance at a mistress and a member of the *demimonde*, Clara did not use her reputation to be unkind. She never had and she would not start now. They might see her disapproval and fussiness as unkindness, but they had failed to notice she did not turn it on those who could not defend themselves.

"How do you do?" Clara asked.

There was a beat of silence before Selene smiled. "Oh, they have underestimated you, haven't they?"

Clara blushed. She actually felt her cheeks go pink. She had never received such a compliment. "Thank you."

"I feel much less concern for your nerves now and can say that I believe you have been placed in the dower house with me." Selene tilted her head. "They'll want you to be shocked over that."

"I'm sure they will."

"But you aren't? You shan't march away in high dudgeon?"

"That depends."

"On what?"

"How loudly do you snore?"

Selene laughed. It was a lovely, sultry sound that had most of the other guests turning their way. Even Bram smiled a little from his post by the door, but he was smiling at Clara.

Half a dozen men straightened their cravats and began to race each other in their direction. "Oh, now you've done it," Clara murmured. "It will be a massacre."

"Never mind," Selene murmured back, her red lips curving. "Your man will save you."

Clara blinked. "He's not my man."

Selene only patted her knee, as though Clara was a silly old woman who'd forgotten her spectacles were already on her nose.

CHAPTER TEN

THE VILLAGE OF Montragroux was clustered around the main square with its medieval stone cross and cobbles underfoot. The blacksmith was already at his work, the steady beat of the hammer like a heartbeat. Acrid smoke wafted. A nearby horse protested with an equine sneeze and an affronted snort. It was a very pretty village, with a grocer, a dressmaker, a bakery, and a shoemaker.

It would have been like any other village were it not for the obvious preparations being made for the Devil's Night.

Round cookies with white frosting and red raspberry nipples. Breadsticks that could only be called…suggestive.

Actually, there was nothing suggestive about it. It was plain for anyone to see. Right there in the window of the bakery, next to the nipple cookies and the pitchfork baguettes. Clara kept her expression of polite disinterest even as she wondered how that could possibly be physically accurate.

A woman in a matronly lace cap and wrinkles that showed her smile bought two. Behind her, the vicar sighed.

And bought three.

Clara nearly giggled. If the vicar planned to eat bread with his supper, there were no other options. Even the hot cross bun looked like…well…*buns*.

She bought a basket of them to give herself something to do

as she eavesdropped. And because they looked delicious. She was offered courteous nods of greetings, sidelong glances at her plain dress, a twist of honey bread to try. But no gossip. Not a single murmur. It was quiet as a tomb until she left the shop.

The mantua maker had a display of masks for the occasion, painted and glued with spangles that caught the light. There were feathers, velvet, silk fringe. The Devil's Night and the accompanying ball, however outrageous, were clearly good for business.

Clara had to remind herself that she was here as a Spinster, not the Nightingale.

Even as she coveted a mask sewn with silver glass beads and crystal drops along the edge. Regretfully, she put it back on the stand. "You do beautiful work," she said.

"Thank you," the shop owner replied over her needle. She was working on something in rose velvet. It shimmered softly like the inside of a shell. "Are you visiting the Hall?"

"Yes, I am. I've never been before."

Two of the other customers exchanged the kind of glance Clara could feel in the back of her eyeballs. She could pinpoint it while blindfolded. At midnight.

She's *a guest at the Hall?*

Clara swallowed but otherwise refused to react. She smiled as though she had no idea what they were whispering, when in actuality she could have written the script for them. Also blindfolded.

Silence thrummed, just as in the bakery.

Ordinarily, one could gain valuable news about the presiding gentry from the local busybodies. The mayor, the wealthiest merchant, a woman who was the cousin of the housekeeper at the Hall. Gossips were the best bet, but even here, where Clara was unknown, she knew it would not do her much good. One look at her dull dress and starched spine and the gossip dried up. No one wanted to be scolded or reminded that they should mind their manners.

Clara didn't either, so she did not blame them.

At any rate, she had made a basic mistake. Priya relied on information brought to her by lady's maids and valets and armies of maidservants. Matilda excelled at gathering gossip from daughters with vendettas. Emmeline knew every countess and duchess by name. But Clara would not get anywhere seeking the most popular villager, the chattiest girl, not even the dressmaker, at whose shop scandals were usually traded over ribbon choices and issues of *La Belle Assemblée*.

None of those were environments where Clara excelled. She looked too…starchy. Proper. And she needed to stop acting as though it was otherwise, or she would never get anywhere. She was following the wrong rules. She was not a charming, dashing lady, nor was she Priya, with her occult abilities to get information from anyone, anywhere.

She *was* Miss Vinegar, like it or not.

She needed someone overlooked. Someone avoided. Someone who had lived in the village for some time. An old woman, preferably.

In other words, a true spinster.

It took two turns around the village before she saw an old woman sitting on a stone wall, scowling at the children playing keep-away with a ball. Her white hair was caught in a soft knot, her shawl wrapped tightly around her. She was knitting socks with daffodil-yellow yarn that she set down in favor of the end of a charred potato. Clara approached her through the long grass.

"Are you in mourning, girl?" the old woman snapped before Clara could say anything.

"No?" *What an odd question.*

"Then you are far too young to be wearing that gray. Makes you look pinched." She snorted. "Youth is wasted on the young."

"I am twenty-nine years old." An old maid, according to the whispers of newly introduced debutantes, barely eighteen.

"I said what I said. Now what do you want, bothering an old woman eating her baked potato in peace?"

"I have hot cross buns from the bakery."

Her interest was piqued and then quickly shoved behind a mask of irritability. "Good for you."

"Would you like one?"

She sniffed. "Bribery."

"Absolutely."

A crack of a laugh. "Finally, my worth is recognized." She preened, just a little, before accepting the hot cross bun and then just taking the whole lot. "Now what do you want?"

"I'm Lady Clara."

"They call me Granny Mab."

"It's a pleasure to make your acquaintance."

A scoff. "Then you should probably get out more, find a hobby. Isn't that what you fine ladies do? Charity and decoupage?"

"I'm a guest up at Eastbourne Hall."

"I figured as much, though you don't look the type."

Clara stifled a sigh. "I know."

"That wasn't an insult, my girl. Despite that horrid dress."

"You are not fond of the Hall?"

"Never been, have I? Someone like me? But I've heard a thing or two."

Something Clara was very much counting on. "You've never been at all?"

"Oh, a few times for harvest suppers in the field, and once to bring my sister her supplies when her courses came unexpectedly. I was a seamstress and sometimes a lace maker." She held up her gnarled fingers. "But my sister worked in the kitchens for the old marquis. He was an odd one too, but kind enough."

"The new marquis is not kind?"

"Not to old women and wallflowers," Granny Mab said drily. "Which I am sure you have already found out yourself. He does not care to have us marring his view or interrupting his pleasures. He likes us out of the way."

"Has he always been like that?"

"He moved half of the village down into the valley so he

could better see the countryside from his balcony." She shrugged. "Bah. Toffs." She squinted an eye at Clara. "You're not the first one to come down here and ask questions about him."

"I'm not?" *Interesting.*

"Nah, some young bloke was asking questions just yesterday."

"And what did you tell him?"

"Nothing. I didn't like his attitude." Granny Mab winked. "He offered me a penny. I prefer hot cross buns."

Clara smiled. "And what would you tell *me* about the marquis? For another basket of hot cross buns?"

"That you should stay far away from him, but you already know that, a clever girl like you."

"How do you know I am clever?" Clara narrowed her eyes. "And don't say it's my dress. It's not *that* bad."

Granny Mab cackled. "You've got that look, is all. Like a governess."

"Splendid," Clara said drily. Some ladies with pale hair and slender bones looked like fairy queens. Not her. But as a transition to the real questions she wanted to ask, she could not find better. "I suppose there is a governess up at the Hall?"

"No, but they had a chaperone until recently." Granny Mab lowered her voice. "She's disappeared."

"Disappeared?"

"She snuck into that house just down the lane, the one with the cracked window. And that was the last we saw of her."

"I see. Is there anything else?" Sybil would not have stopped in an abandoned cottage without very good reason. And she would not have let herself be seen if she did not want to.

Granny Mab raised her eyebrows shrewdly. "Does the baker have any of those bubby cookies left? The ones with the jam?"

"I can check." The nipple cookies were popular, apparently.

"Good. He won't let me inside anymore, says I steal. Me!"

Given the holes in her shawl and the state of her mended dress, Clara would not have blamed her. In fact, she was going to buy an extra loaf of the dark bread that lasted longer than sugared buns. And a wheel of cheese. Surely there was somewhere to buy cheese in the village? Even if it was carved into the shape of a naked nymph.

"Thank you," Clara said. She didn't know what any of it meant yet, but it was more than she'd had to work with just a quarter of an hour ago. "Is there anything else I can get you?"

"One of those beers from the inn."

Clara brought her two.

On her way back up the road that cut through the village, she saw a circulating library wagon with books wrapped in paper and string. She wondered if anyone had stopped by the Golden Griffin to ask about the newest Nightingale chapbook. If there would be enough money to buy meat and more coal if the weather did not stay warm. If this was her last chapbook to be published. Given the threatening note tucked into her cuff, it might well be.

Sadness and fury twined through her. She had wanted to burn the note on principle, but getting rid of evidence would not her help her in the long run.

"No reason for that girl to go into that cottage," Granny Mab said, wiping foam from her mouth with the back of her gnarled hand after taking a mouthful that would have felled a man twice her size and half her age.

"Why not?"

"Well, they found that Welsh girl down there one morning, in her nightdress and bare feet. She was frantic. Caught some fever, they said when they came to fetch her. She howled something fierce."

"Which Welsh girl?" Clara asked.

"Yardley, Yarffyd. Some Frenchie name as well. Blanche?"

"Miss Blanche Yarwood?"

"Aye, that's the one. Merchant's daughter or some such."

"When was this?"

"Oh, two months now? There was snow on the ground. No one dared go near."

"And did she recover?"

"Could be. Haven't seen her since."

"I see."

Clara tried not to be obvious when she left Granny Mab and made a beeline straight for the cottage.

"Well, what have we here?"

Clara whirled around to find Bram leaning against a tree, arms crossed.

He did not sound happy to see her.

CHAPTER ELEVEN

HE DID NOT *look* happy either.

In fact, he was rapidly crossing from irritation to banked fury right before her very eyes. She blinked at him. "Has something happened?"

"Yes."

She blinked again when he did not elaborate. He was not a very forthcoming man, as it turned out. It was not a surprise, mind you. She had spoken to him more in the last few days than in the last few months combined. Including the night she'd jumped out of a window into his arms. Which they had never spoken about, not once.

His gaze roamed over her as if he were assuring himself she was well. She tried not to tingle, she really did. "Captain Thorn?" she prodded.

"You left."

"Yes. And?"

"And you promised not to leave without me."

Someone should tell him that if he wanted to be more intimidating, he should not look quite so handsome when he glowered. But it wasn't going to be her. Not when she should not find him so handsome in the first place.

And there was *some* trepidation. His glower was very…honed. But she was more intrigued at her body's response.

If she hadn't been enjoying the little tremors, she might have considered taking notes. For science. For literature.

It was important to be accurate, after all. She had a duty to her readers.

And to the curious heat nibbling at her.

"It's not safe," Bram insisted.

She nearly laughed. He was right about that. There was nothing safe about his effect on her. "It's the middle of the day," she pointed out before she said something completely out of line. "In a sleepy English village."

Missing women notwithstanding.

And where a pretend chaperone may or may not have gone missing just before the most notorious social event of the country, one that routinely ended in duels, ruination, lost inheritances. Occasionally murder.

"It's not safe," he repeated, and it was a fair point. The early spring light touched the silver threaded through his dark hair, glimmered in his neat beard. It was deeply unfashionable to sport a beard. She had no idea why. She suddenly could not imagine writing a hero without one.

"Don't you want to know what I've found out?" she asked.

"What I want is to turn you over my knee."

Clara wasn't sure which of them was more surprised by his statement. It pinged between them, electric.

And then those calm shutters closed over his face. He was the enigmatic captain once more, all authority and quiet competence. She could not read his expression, no matter how she tried.

As an expert at hiding her true feelings, it was galling.

Especially as she was quite certain *her* cheeks were bright pink. Her breathing was not quite even either. And when had it become so hot? The last of the hoarfrost threatened to melt under her feet.

"Go on, then," he said roughly.

For a wild, heated moment she thought he was suggesting she lift her skirts and bend over his thighs so he might spank her.

More shocking yet, she considered it. For a great deal longer than she probably ought to.

"We're not the only ones asking about the marquis," she croaked.

"Not a surprise, I suppose, with an occasion such as this one. Everyone wants leverage. He's got more enemies than friends, I reckon. Should be useful."

She swallowed, her throat dry, her wits discombobulated. "The *chaperone* had a jaunt through the village before she disappeared."

Bram stilled, the way a hawk might sensing his luncheon sporting in the fields. Pity the poor rabbit. "Did she, now?"

"Just down the way there, where another girl was running wild with a fever. And no one has seen her since. I'm on my way to investigate."

"Alone."

She smiled, because they were safe under a tree where no one would whisper about her behind their fans. And because he made her want to smile, with that glower, the arch of his brow. "Not anymore."

He grunted.

Amiably, she liked to think. It felt like a sonnet.

The abandoned cottage, on the other hand, was a ghost story full of warning. It was wattle and daub with a thatched roof and a red door hanging crookedly off its hinges. Dandelions bloomed in a tangle under the window. A black dove had been scratched into the doorpost.

"And who told you Miss Taunton came down this way?" Bram asked.

"Granny Mab."

He looked briefly flummoxed. "Granny Mab."

"Yes, for a basket of pastries."

"Now *he's* better than decoupage!" Granny Mab hollered as she ambled past. Her timing was impeccable. She ought to have been on the stage.

"*That* Granny Mab, in point of fact."

He just shook his head. "I'll go in first."

"Do you expect to find pirates or French soldiers?" Clara asked archly. "It's just an old cottage. I don't expect Sybil to be hiding out in there."

She stayed close behind him. This was her investigation, after all. He halted on the doorstep. She bounced right off his wide back with an "oomph."

"All right back there?" he asked, amused.

She rubbed the tip of her nose. The man must be made of stone. And why did he smell so good, like lime candies? "I'm fine."

"I said I was going in first."

"And there you are, first."

He huffed a sigh. "You're supposed to wait out here until I give the all-clear."

"I *am* waiting out here."

He turned, closed his large hands around her shoulders, and lifted her bodily off the ground. Her toes dangled. Their gazes collided. That electricity again, a current of awareness prickling between them. She could practically taste it on her tongue like the most decadent of chocolates. The moment lasted longer than was strictly necessary. Hot, hungry, and strangely prophetic.

His jaw twitched.

And then he deposited her very gently back on the ground, several feet away from the front door. She was practically across the street. "This is ridiculous."

"If you put yourself in danger, I really will put you over my knee," he muttered.

She flushed, head to toe. No one much cared about her safety and comfort. She was not someone who was automatically considered. Certainly, she was not someone who was teased and flirted with. Was he even flirting with her? He had muttered it as though she was not supposed to hear.

Which just made it better, for some reason. She felt it in her breasts and the intimate flesh between her thighs, suddenly hot and thrumming with awareness.

"All right now," Bram said from the doorway. "No pirates."

And yet she felt thoroughly plundered.

She nearly giggled. Miss Vinegar did *not* giggle.

Bram's expression softened, but it was so brief she might have imagined it. She crossed the dirt road and followed him inside, her pulse beating thickly in her throat, her belly, her puckered nipples. She closed her pelisse tighter, willing herself not to act like a goose. Even as she wondered if he would mind very much if she fashioned her next hero after him. Made him do wicked things. Delicious things.

"Are you giggling?" Bram asked, turning to stare at her.

"Certainly not," she replied primly. "I do not giggle."

He stepped closer, his words brushing the hair at her temple. "You don't fool me, Lady Clara," he said softly, with a dark kind of knowing. "You never did."

She might have forgotten how to breathe. Breathing was not important. What was important was the nearness of him, the warmth of his body, the desperate heat climbing up her thighs. The fact that she might actually die if she did not get closer still. How did he kiss a woman? Softly? Leisurely? Forcefully?

She'd written a dozen kisses. But she'd never written his.

She licked her lower lip. She couldn't help it.

"I told you not to do that," he warned.

"Do what?"

He huffed a small chuckle, but there was nothing light or amused about it. It was rough, tempting. "And I told you already that you don't fool me."

And wasn't that amazing?

Dangerous, definitely. But amazing too.

She swayed a little closer, mesmerized. Then she snapped back to her regular posture.

"What will it take, I wonder?" he asked. "For you to let go."

"I'm sure I don't know what you mean." She cleared her

throat. "We have work to do."

"Of course, Lady Clara."

She narrowed her eyes at him, felt needled without knowing exactly why. Something about the way that he used her title. "Look for anything untoward," she said with what was alarmingly close to a flounce.

She inspected the cottage as though she was a stalk of dry winter wheat and Bram was fire, circling her warily, always alert to exactly where he was in relation to her. She decided it meant she would have made a marvelous spy. Aware, conscientious. A dismal flirt, but a marvelous spy.

The cottage held a kitchen table by the smoke-darkened stone hearth, two chairs, a shelf for plates and cups and bowls. A narrow bed with a moth-eaten blanket and a wooden chest at the foot.

And little black doves everywhere.

Clearly, Sybil had not felt safe. Just as clearly, she had only been able to leave maddening clues.

Clara peered under the mattress and in the wooden chest. Bram crouched down to feel up the flue of the hearth for anything hidden there. They found spiders and pencils and doilies. No obvious pleas for help, no letters accusing the marquis of nefarious deeds. No convenient map to Sybil's location. Not even a single lock that fit the key around Clara's neck.

She let out a disgruntled sigh. "Priya would have found something more by now."

"Priya is a witch."

"I'm going to tell her you said that."

"She already knows she's a witch. I've told her."

"She probably ought to have come herself. We don't even know what we are looking for."

"We'll find something."

"How can you be so sure?" she asked. Sybil's wellbeing was in their hands. As was Heloise's.

"The marquis is up to his eyeballs in misdeeds—there's

bound to be something useful."

"Perhaps."

The small cottage smelled like wood smoke and dust. Sunlight streamed through the window, a wash of pale gold. There was a vase of dried flowers on the sill, a basket of mending beneath it. "I like it better here than at the Hall—is that very odd of me?" she asked.

"Eastbourne Hall currently looks as though a brothel threw up on a circus. Nobody needs that much gilt or red velvet. And even the drapes are soaked in perfume."

"It's very striking by candlelight."

"In the daylight it makes my eyeballs itch."

She smiled. She couldn't help it.

"So, no, it does not make you odd," he continued. "I feel the same way."

"I think that just means we're both odd," she pointed out.

"Perhaps." He was smiling again when he said it, just a bit.

She followed the trail of little black birds, hastily painted. They flew over the rafters, along the headboard, across the windowsill. There were eight in all, but she had no idea if that meant anything.

The little blue bird painted on the edge of the stone at the foot of the hearth definitely meant something. Especially as the stone was just loose enough to pry free.

Underneath: dirt, a startled spider.

And another key.

This one was different than the first, longer, with scrollwork.

They checked again to make sure there was nothing else hidden away that the lock might open, floorboards that could be pried up, hollow table legs. There was not. Only more dust, a mouse nest, and splinters. Clara drew her hand away from the underside of the rough table with a sharp inhale. Bram was instantly at her side. "Just a splinter," she said, taking off her half-glove, which was now torn. She tried to work it free, but it was too deep. "Some detective I am," she added drily.

"Let me see," Bram demanded.

"It's nothing," she said, but he was already reaching for her.

He scowled at her tiny wound as though she had been shot through with a musket. She curled her fingers into her palm, but he wouldn't let her. He brushed his thumb over the end of the splinter, too small to grasp, but just sharp enough to make her wince. He immediately stopped. "I'm sorry."

"It's just a pinch. I'm sure it will work itself out eventually."

He shook his head stubbornly. "It comes out now, and then we'll wash it when we get back to the Hall. The smallest wounds fester."

"Are there a lot of splinter-related injuries on ships?" she asked, half joking.

"The splinters from cannon strikes can be as serious as any other weapons. They might easily take out eyes, fester in limbs, shred a sailor to ribbons."

"This is hardly that. No explosions. Just a little dust." Had he received his scars from cannon fire? "Is it rotten boards that make it so dangerous? Or do enemies paint noxious substances on the canon balls before they fire them?"

"They do not." His mouth quirked. "But they should. The Royal Navy should take you on as an advisor."

"Priya is the one with the poisons."

"And yet you're the one to watch." He lifted her hand and—before she could wonder if he meant to dig it out with a knife or a needle, and why he had such things on his person—sucked her finger into his mouth.

The feeling took her entirely by surprise. His tongue ran over her skin, and then he sucked her fingertip harder into his warm mouth. There were answering tingles in her throat, her belly, knees. There was a single jolt between her thighs, and she nearly gasped. His eyes met hers, flaring blue as the heart of a flame. She swallowed when he sucked harder, then soothed her with this tongue.

He slowly released her, finally looking away. "There," he said hoarsely, pulling the rest of the splinter free.

It was work to swallow and find her voice. "Thank you."

CHAPTER TWELVE

B RAM NEEDED A moment to get himself under control, not to
mention get his bearings. There were too many warnings in
that cottage, too many of those dammed black doves. Missing
girls, keys.

And something else.

There.

The glint of sun on a gold button.

A man waited, crouched on the roof of the vicarage. Waited
for him. For them? For Clara?

Like hell.

Was it one of the marquis's men watching the cottage? Why?
It didn't matter. He would not get even a glimpse of Clara. Bram
would burn the village down first. And Eastbourne Hall. The
fields all the way to sea that lay some distance from Hampshire.

It was bad enough that she was walking through the house,
ignoring the snide remarks of people who did not deserve to
stand in her shadow. He had made that clear, at the very least.
Clear enough that Lord Faltingham had remembered a prior
engagement.

In Ireland.

Bram had not sent him there personally in a leaky rowboat,
for which he definitely deserved a medal. Never mind his naval
gold medal. This was even more important.

He could not fathom why everyone was so blind to the real Clara peeking out behind the plain dresses and the stoic expressions. A devil hid within the spinster. One who was incongruously comfortable chatting with a courtesan, curious and surprisingly accepting. She had a sense of humor, a keen eye. Resolve.

She had even *giggled*.

He'd never felt prouder than in that moment. She had lowered her shields in front of him. Just a little. But he would not lower his. Not for a single second. The Devil's Night was bad enough. It attracted all kinds of powerful people with more money than principles. The marquis was something worse.

Clara was in danger every second she was inside that house. It ate at him. But she was no safer here.

"Out the back," he ordered, ushering her past the kitchen table and the narrow bed to a window. He yanked it open, sweeping for danger. It would have been more effective from the bird's nest of his ship, but he would make do. A muddy lane, three white geese waddling happily, a privy at the end of the garden.

Clara tilted her head. "You want to climb out the window?"

"I want *you* to climb out the window," he corrected her. "Quickly."

She frowned as if getting ready to argue, saw something in his face, thank Christ, and relented. "Very well."

"When you get your feet on the ground, you run as fast as you can for that little copse of trees there, understand?"

She nodded, bending to knot her skirts between her knees, like a set of makeshift trousers. He caught a glimpse of ankle, strong calves.

If only there was time to linger. He would have done so for hours.

Even if she was not for him. An earl's daughter and a captain a decade her senior with more scars than social graces. He still felt the swell of the waves under his feet, even landlocked for the past year. He didn't dance. He'd never driven a barouche. His cravats weren't starched.

Not that any of it mattered. All that mattered was getting her away from here.

Clara swung her leg nimbly over the sill, using the chair to boost herself up. "Why am I always crawling through windows around you?"

As if he needed reminding of the abject terror that had seized him watching her clinging to the side of a Mayfair townhouse in the freezing sleet, with no one to help her.

He still woke up sweating over it.

"Ready?" he asked, dividing his focus between the front door and the window.

She wriggled out, dropping to the ground with a little huff of an exclamation. He ducked down to watch her run, his dagger in his hand. The gray of her dress helped hide her in the trees. He exhaled when she was safely ensconced.

And then he turned back to the front door, marching outside with a certain violence in his heart.

⟫⟩✕⟨⟪

CLARA DID NOT need a flock of black doves carved into the walls to know there was a problem.

She also knew that this was a *most* inappropriate time to sigh over the clench of a man's jaw or the glint of cold determination in his eye. The contradiction of that with the gentle way he touched her, making sure she would not catch herself on a stray nail or another jagged sliver of wood—it made her brain stutter. Her insides flutter.

All things that might be quite enjoyable were she not now crouched in the bushes, wondering what was happening to Bram. She frowned at a bee bumbling toward a patch of dandelions. Bram surely should have popped back around to find her by now.

What was he doing? Why had he been so adamant that she sneak out the back? The marquis was hardly likely to be taking a stroll through the village looking for victims.

Bram was setting himself up as the bait. And she had let him.

Idiot.

She straightened, emerging from the foliage. One of the geese caught sight of her and squawked. "Hush," she muttered, even though geese were not known for their willingness to be hushed.

She stepped out onto the muddy lane, a branch of blooming lilac in her hand. It wasn't much of a sword. It would have to do. She crept past another cottage before coming to a grassy lane running toward the street. She kept her back to the building, feeling very daring. This was something Peony might do. Or Emmeline.

Someone who was not acerbic and rule bound. Someone Bram could count on.

Someone trailing geese.

One of them pecked the weeds very near her foot. Too near. She stifled a squeak, waving her sword of purple blossoms, but kept her gaze on the street, on the shadow cast by the church, a cat licking his paw on a front step.

On Bram grappling with a man.

She suddenly had no idea what Peony or Emmeline might do in this situation. But she had a stick and some geese who would not be hushed. Who were known to be territorial. Their reputation was even fiercer than Priya's.

Excellent.

Because she did not care for the way the stranger was trying to stab Bram in the chest.

Bollocks to that.

Bram was holding his own, no question. He was steady and deft on his feet, in the way only a man used to being at sea could be. There one moment, adjusting the next. Only he was not factoring wind speed or rough waves, but the attack of a man who might not be as wide as him, but was just as tall. Meaning his reach was equal. A lucky hit was entirely possible.

Not on Clara's watch.

Bram avoided a slash at his midsection from a long knife whose blade did not look the least bit hygienic.

Clara had a disapproving glare and three geese in her arsenal.

Geese.

"I will bring you grapes. Or caterpillars." What did geese eat? "You are very brave soldiers. Onward! Save the day!"

She waved her branch at them, feeling both ridiculous and a little guilty.

"Beg your pardon," she said when one of them made a very affronted noise. "But this is your village—are you going to let that man there make a bigger fuss than you? The other geese will mock you."

She herded them forward, stamping her feet until they exploded in a furious flurry of feathers and beaks and screams better suited to a gothic novel. Right into street, startling the cat, who yowled. And knocking over a clay pot, smashing it into bits.

A woman came to the door, wiping her hands. "Alice, mind your bloody geese!"

"Your cat is the one who broke my pot!"

Someone else added their opinion from a second-floor window. It was not favorable.

And, all in all, far too much attention for a surprise assassination outside the vicarage.

Take that, villain.

The man cut his losses, turning on his heel and sprinting away.

"Keep running!" Clara shouted after him. She threw her branch of lilac flowers for good measure. She'd had no idea how vengeful she truly was.

Bram swore and then turned to stare at her. But she was not done with her vengeance. She darted after the villain, making it two steps before a solid arm clamped around her stomach and lifted her off her feet. "Are you daft, woman?" Bram snarled in her ear.

"He tried to stab you!"

"I told you to hide."

"I did hide."

"For all of three minutes!"

"And look how much trouble you got into in those three minutes!" She crossed her arms, still dangling. It somewhat ruined the effect. "You're welcome."

He muttered something under his breath. She did not ask him to repeat it, as it did not sound complimentary.

"You seem agitated, Captain Thorn."

He set her down, jaw ticking. "You'll bloody well stay right here." He stormed away after the stranger, who had headed toward the inn.

Naturally, Clara followed.

CHAPTER THIRTEEN

T HE INN HAD been an inn since before the time of Queen Elizabeth. It was built of dark wood that tilted considerably to the left. The thatched roof, on the other hand, sagged in the middle. Starlings sang from the straw. It was lovely and welcoming in its own way. Or would have been had a stranger not just stolen the last horse from the stable yard and left in its place a coldly furious captain home from a decade at war with the French.

Bram did not posture or berate anyone—he merely asked clipped questions, his eyes deadly. It was a very effective combination.

It did not, however, have the power to produce a horse out of thin air.

"Sorry, sir," one of the stable hands said, eyes wide. Behind him, the stable master was threatening everyone within earshot. The inn was a stopping point for wealthy guests who did not have rooms at the Hall. Their horses were worth more than the entire inn. It was only chance that had the stables empty, and the mounts already claimed by their owners for the day. "We only have the one mule, and she'll bite you before every step."

"Which way did the thief go?" Bram asked.

"Headed east toward the crossroads."

Bram nodded. He did not glance back at Clara. "I thought I

told you to stay there."

"I did not listen," she said crisply. "As I am not your dog."

"That's not what I meant, and you know it," he muttered.

"I am also not one of your officers."

"What happened to the very reserved spinster who does not like to make waves?"

"She is otherwise occupied."

He almost smiled. "Come on, then."

"Where are we going?" she asked, hurrying to match his long strides. She would learn to fly before she asked him to slow down.

"There's an old ruin in the fields just back there. It has a decent tower, and I should be able to get a better view from there." His eyes found hers. "Keep up."

Keep up was perhaps the most romantic thing anyone had ever said to her.

She was more accustomed to *Oh no, not her again* and *I suppose we can invite her if we must.*

Clara kept up.

While Bram's strides ate up the countryside, Clara's stride resembled more of a hop, something reminiscent of a demented bunny. It was not easy work to clamber over hillocks of frozen earth and mounds of tangled grass slick with melted frost. She did not utter a single sound of protest or effort. Not a one.

Bram reached back and caught her hand when she teetered as she clambered over the low stone wall. He did not glance back, did not otherwise appear to have remembered she was there. But his hand was there when she needed, steadying, a quick help and then they were off again.

The ruins were very near the edge of the village, a run-down medieval castle used by the local family before they built the more modern Eastbourne Hall. There was the memory of a moat circling the bailey, walls that used to encompass a courtyard, stables, work buildings. And then another small hill and a wall with an empty window soaring to a point and the remains of the tower. Stairs marched up the side, half worn away and open to the air. Ivy had claimed everything in between.

Bram was already halfway up the tower, sure-footed and determined. Clara picked her way carefully and cautiously. One didn't become a different person overnight, after all. And she had no intention of becoming an idiot.

When she caught up with him, Bram's boots were planted firmly, the wind tugging at his dark hair and his coat. His narrowed gaze swept the waves of grass, the undulation of the hills, like that of any good captain. "Stay close to the wall," he said tightly. "It's not particularly safe up here."

"Do you see him?" Clara asked. The wind was colder up here and made her eyes water.

Bram rubbed his beard, the only sign of his frustration. "He took the road headed to Fitcher, I imagine. It's the closest town proper. Even were I to magically secure a horse in the next five minutes, he'll lose himself there."

"You did not recognize him?"

"No. He wore a scarf over his face. He has red hair, though, I think."

"That's something."

"Not nearly enough to go on."

"I suppose not. So what now?"

"Now I get you back to the Hall. And I'm still angry that you came out here alone and, worse yet, did not stay put when I told you to hide."

"I had my geese."

He glanced at her out of the corner of his eye. "You should not be enjoying this."

"I've never really been on an adventure."

"Your feet are wet. March is not a good month for an adventure."

"They will dry."

Another sidelong glance. "Where did you learn that trick with the geese?"

"They were already cross. I just directed them a little." The sun was warm on her hair, and she realized she must have lost her bonnet somewhere between the geese and the tower and had not noticed.

She hated bonnets. And she'd never dared be without one. Freckles, sun spots. Wrinkles.

She decided she might like a freckle or two. Maybe a dozen.

The fichu she had added to her dress was too warm under the sun, and she took it off. Miss Vinegar without her fichu. She'd already formed an army of geese—what did one more transgression matter?

Bram watched her, throat bobbing as he swallowed. Had she shocked him? A man who was just assaulted by a stranger interrupted by a bunch of homicidal geese was surely made of sterner stuff. Unless he had been injured?

She stopped, frowning at him.

He stopped too, frowning back. "What?"

"That man tried to stab you." She sounded outraged even to her own ears. Everything had happened so fast that she hadn't really had the time to process.

Bram just shrugged, as if that sort of thing happened all of the time. The thought made a hard, cold seed take root in her belly. She didn't like it. She didn't like it one bit. She yanked his coat open. It was very unseemly of her.

Miss Vinegar would have a case of the vapors.

Bram only raised one eyebrow. The one with the tiny, faded scar running through it. Someone else had tried to stab him, maybe. Or one of those large splinters he'd mentioned had caught him.

She did not care for that either.

"Did he hurt you?"

"Him?" Bram snorted, mildly insulted. "Barely nicked one of my buttons. And I think that was an accident."

"He cut a hole in your peacoat!" She seized his arm, glaring at the offending slash through the navy wool. "Did he cut you? Are you wounded?"

"Clara," he said calmly, almost fondly. "I'm fine. Not even a scratch."

"Oh." And here she was clutching at him like a ninny. She dropped his arm as if it were on fire. Truthfully, she didn't so much as drop it as toss it away. What happened to her much-lauded decorum when she was around this man? Honestly, it was embarrassing. "You're very nonchalant for someone who was so fretful over a little splinter."

"I wasn't fretful," he grumbled.

She couldn't help but tease him a little. "Cross?" she suggested. "Peevish? Distraught?"

He glanced down at her. "I don't remember you talking to anyone else like this."

"I don't," she said. And wasn't that delightful?

"I had it on good authority that you were a reserved, proper lady of impeccable bearing."

"I do sound about as exciting a tepid water, don't I?" she asked drily. "Perhaps you are a bad influence on me."

She hadn't *meant* to make that sound suggestive, nor to immediately imagine all the ways in which he might indeed prove himself a bad influence. Against a wall. In a carriage. From above. From behind.

She had to clear her throat to get her breath back. A modicum of propriety. It helped that she had practice in that respect.

It did *not* help that he looked intrigued. Not shocked. Not disdainful or derisive.

Intrigued.

She felt it in the back of her knees, in her thighs, which went warm and soft. *She* was more than intrigued.

"I admit he got in a punch," he said as they crossed through a field of purple crocuses leading to the side gardens. Swallows dipped and dove overhead. He rubbed his jaw.

She turned to him, wide eyed. "He did?"

"I'd tell you he punches like my grandmother, but Nan has a

wicked left hook even now."

She smiled, itching to ask him questions about said grandmother. She didn't dare, in case he asked questions back. She had too many secrets. And he already seemed to see her more than anyone ever had in her entire life. Better not to say anything at all.

She took the key from her pocket as they crossed the fields, the sun warm on her shoulders. "This could open anything," she said, disgruntled. "Anywhere."

"Best guess still has it opening something in Eastbourne Hall."

"Which narrows it down to over a hundred rooms."

"Exactly. Nothing to it."

He stopped to help her climb the step stile between two fenced fields. The grass was thick with marsh marigolds and coltsfoot, liberally sprinkled with dandelions. "If he *is* hiding something behind a locked door, why would he risk having such a grand affair as this? With guests overrunning his estate?" Clara mused.

"Misdirection? Not to mention that the arrogance of the aristocracy is unparalleled," Bram said drily. "And most toffs who consider themselves fashionable or powerful want a turn hosting a Devil's Night. Lord knows Devil does not let anyone onto his estate, if they could even find it. He's not about to host it."

"Why do you think he does it?"

"Power. Revenge. Love. One or all three. I don't like that it's another factor in this whole mess with Sybil."

"Maybe we can use it to our advantage."

"The Devil's Night always has the advantage," he said. "Remember that."

"But it's what we're both here for." To find their friend. They both worked for the Spinster Society. It was silly of her to have hoped, even for a moment, that there was another reason. She really must rein in her imagination. She was not a character in one of her own stories, much as she might like to be sometimes.

She was simply Lady Clara.

"I'm here for you," he insisted. "To keep you safe."

"Why?" she asked plainly.

"What?"

"You heard me. Why? Why would care about keeping me safe?"

"You are alone."

Pride drew her up, snapped her spine straight. He wasn't wrong, and it was nothing to be ashamed of.

Still. She had her books and the Spinsters. It was more than many people had. She did not want his pity.

She wanted so much more.

What a time to admit it to herself. She forced a smile. "Thank you, Captain Thorn."

He frowned as she moved around him and into the chatter of the house party garden. "What just happened?"

CHAPTER FOURTEEN

THE LADY'S MAID who came to help Clara get ready for the evening was frazzled and overworked. She smiled but looked as though she had not slept in days. Margaret was tall, with a tidy uniform and a basket of supplies for hairstyles and cosmetics. She was also slightly out of breath and had likely already been helping ladies with their corsets and hair tongs for hours now. Clara caught the longing glance she sent toward the direction of her tea tray.

Mrs. Meadows continued to make good on her promise and had clearly decided that feeding Bram was going to be her new mission. Clara had never seen so much cheese. The trays never stopped arriving. There three types of scones at minimum, preserves, honey, and cake. Sometimes cucumber salad, always meat pies of one kind or another. Always tins of shortbread.

Margaret curtsied a greeting. "Lady Clara, what should you like? Ringlets? Rouge?"

Clara smiled. As if she could wear rouge. She would like to one day. It would be nice to not always be the color of porridge. "If you could help me with my stays, that would be lovely. I can manage my own hair."

There was not much to manage, very little frippery, no soft curls or clever twists. Maragret's expression said as much. "Of course, my lady."

"I do have some questions for you."

"Oh?" she said noncommittally, coming to tie Clara's corset laces and help her with her gown in less time than it would have taken for Clara to pour her a cup of tea.

"Impressive," Clara murmured. "But you must be tired. There are dozens and dozens of ladies here, and they could not all have traveled with their own maids."

"House parties are busy," Margaret agreed. "Not that I'm complaining."

"Of course not—I only mean to say your time is valuable, and I shouldn't wish to overextend you. Why don't you sit and have some tea while I do my own hair?"

"In exchange for what?" Margaret asked suspiciously, even as she edged toward the chair and the promised tea.

"Oh, you're a clever one." Clara grinned. "That will make this much easier." She waved for Margaret to help herself. "Have more honey. I only want to know about Miss Taunton," she said. "She is my cousin and I have not seen her in some time, but apparently she is off to the seaside with the marquis's ward. Unfortunate timing on both our parts."

Margaret paused with her cup on the way to her mouth, but only for a moment. "Yes."

"Do you know her well?"

"A little. She did mention a cousin, actually."

"I'm glad. It's been some time. She had pigtails last we saw each other. Is she happy in her post, do you think?" That was something a cousin would ask, wasn't it?

"I think so, though it's very staid for someone so…"

"Spirited?" Clara suggested, grinning. Sybil was Sybil. "When we were little, she once dressed a duke's donkey in his favorite frock coat, embroidered in Italy. He wept." That was two months ago, actually. And that duke had deserved it.

Margaret's smile softened, became more natural. She helped herself to an iced currant bun. "That sounds like her. However did she become a chaperone?"

"I'm afraid she had a falling-out with her father and had to find her own way in the world."

"She did—does—take great care with Lady Heloise," Margaret said. Clara caught the slip and wanted to pounce on it but restrained herself. "The marquis does not like for her to go far. He worries about her."

"I see. That must be difficult for a young lady." Clara added one more pin to her hair, keeping her eye on Margaret in the looking glass. "He must be used to it, after welcoming Miss Yarwood in his house as well. I've not met her."

"She had a fever and went to Brighton for her lungs."

"I wonder if that's where my cousin went as well. Does he have a house there?"

"I do not know, my lady."

"Ah well, little matter." It did not *feel* like a little matter. "Could you tell me which is Miss Taunton's bedroom? I should like to leave her a gift I brought."

"She took the governess's old quarters up in the nursery."

Not the rooms in the guest wing, as she'd been told. The ones that had felt wrong and strangely empty.

Interesting.

"She left you something, Miss," Margaret added. She pulled a key from her basket.

Another blasted key.

"Thank you, Margaret, that's very helpful."

In theory.

CLARA TOOK A detour on the way to the drawing room. If her calculations were correct, as well as her perusal of old drawings of the Hall, the locked door in the secret passageway led somewhere in this direction. Past the conservatory, not quite as far as the ballroom.

A closed door, right where she had predicted it should be, if the corridor did not simply go on and on. Also a possibility.

This one held more weight. For one thing, her new key fit the lock. Turned with a satisfying click. Even the handle moved.

But the door still did not open.

Clara arrived at the drawing room in a white ball gown like every other white ball gown she had ever worn: simple and unremarkable. She could have been a debutante or a dowager for all of the personality it had.

But underneath, her stocking ribbons were the very prettiest red silk.

Always.

It was important to remind herself that Miss Vinegar was a camouflage, lest she turn into her truly. It was a definite danger. But Miss Vinegar would not wear red silk. The Nightingale would refuse to wear anything else. Somewhere in between, Clara made her stand.

Selene, naturally, wore a gown *entirely* of red silk. No wonder everyone whispered that she must be the Nightingale.

Clara glided through the ballroom, currently set up with gaming tables for those who wished to practice before Devil's Night. Peacock feathers sprouted from the flower arrangement, some gilded and taller than her. The chandeliers glittered over card tables, welcoming players to vingt-et-un, whist, macao. Wagers were placed on the roll of a single die—extraordinarily high wagers, too many of which came down to unwed daughters to pay.

She could not help the purse of her lips. Lord Whitlow sneered back at her.

The room was loud with laughter and shouts and music, thick with the burning of beeswax candles and perfume. Not even remotely tempting. Honestly, Clara would have preferred a book in the library.

And she would cut off her own arm before admitting that to anyone here. Not that they did not already think it. Which was hardly the point.

She felt Bram's eyes on her as she took a turn about the room, more interested in noting which doors had locks, which cabinet drawers, which decorative marble-topped tables. Sybil might have hidden anything anywhere.

By the time Clara reached the end of the long ballroom, Bram had made his way to her side. He did not gleam or glitter, and yet he drew her eye far more easily than a hundred gold feathers under a hundred crystal chandeliers. "You do not look impressed," he remarked.

She wrinkled her nose. "Another reason I am not generally invited to such festivities."

"Do you want to be?"

"Everyone wants to be invited," she said with a tiny shrug to offset the strange, unwelcome heaviness in her chest. "Even if one does not want to attend."

A footman passed right by her without offering her a flute of champagne adorned with a single strawberry. Even the footmen took one look at her and knew.

She tried, once more, to take it as a compliment on her skills at disguise, and was only half successful. Still, she had made this particular bed and there was no sense in feeling sorry for herself.

Bram raised an eyebrow. "I have only ever seen that expression on sailors heading into a hurricane."

"Me?" Clara laughed softly. "I am hardly the hurricane type."

He snorted dubiously.

He might as well have recited a poem with the way she reacted. A tingle, a flush of heat. A ridiculous urge to giggle. Fix her hair. Flash a red silk ribbon.

"Lady Clara," Selene called from the nearby card table. "I am quite outnumbered." She was indeed surrounded by gentlemen in various stages of inebriation. "Will you play?"

"That one?" Lord Whitlow laughed. "She's more likely to deliver you a sermon."

Selene's smile did not slip, but her eyes changed. "Well, that sounds like a challenge, my lord. And we do never back down from a challenge. Do we, Lady Clara?"

Clara swallowed.

Lord Whitlow laughed again. "The virgin and the wh—" He abruptly cut off when Bram loomed. He really was an excellent loomer. She was fairly certain they did not teach that in the navy. It was an innate skill.

"Beg your pardon," he said stonily. He all but seethed with the promise of an avalanche burying an entire village without warning. "I am sure you meant to offer the lady your seat."

Lord Whitlow looked like he was going to protest, decided he was not quite that drunk, or that brave, and promptly abandoned the field. Clara took the offered seat, suddenly very, very willing to go to outright war on behalf of Selene and Bram.

Even if the war was only across a card table decorated with yellow roses.

Interest prickled around them. The courtesan and the spinster. The virgin and the whore. Guests abandoned their own games, lured by the promise of something new. Their boredom might be different than hers, but it was still boredom. Even here, even now.

Selene slid her champagne over to Clara. "Fortification."

Clara took a sip, feeling Bram take up the space behind her chair. A looming, comforting presence.

"Are you any good?" Selene asked.

Clara blinked innocently. "I'm afraid I wouldn't know."

Snickers moved around the circle of spectators. Clara knew the exact moment they reached Bram. A stutter of silence. She did not know which of his glowers he was employing, but it must be formidable indeed.

"How about a game of Brag?" Lord Howell suggested with a wink. "Don't worry, we'll take it easy on you, Lady Clara."

"Thank you, Lord Howell."

Bram's hand closed over the back of her chair, just close enough that she could brush against his knuckles. If she needed to. Wanted to.

She felt the amusement from the other players, from the audience. Bram did not seem amused at all. Selene did, but not at her. It made a flicker of competitiveness flare within.

The cards were dealt, and Clara could not help but notice their beauty—they were hand-painted with intricate details. Slightly wicked details, of course. One of the ladies smiled at her, showing a lot of sharp teeth, waiting for Clara to succumb to a fit of the vapors over a pair of painted buttocks. Or three.

As Clara had written about a moment of passion between three lovers in a similar position, she did not even blink. In fact, she liked to think she could have given the artist some constructive criticism.

The game began, and Clara gathered information as best she could. Lord Howell took a sip of port when he was trying to hide his satisfaction with his cards. Clara might not know Lord St. John well, but his wife touched the diamonds around her neck nervously when he refused another card. Selene drew attention to her rather splendid cleavage with every hand.

Clara was having *fun*. Most of the people around her expected her to be sour or scandalized. She was neither.

She was *winning*.

All because they thought they knew her and did not consider for one moment that they might be wrong. Did not think to look a little deeper. All weapons in the hands of a Spinster. She wanted so desperately to lay her cards down. To hear them choke. She knew it would sound like angels singing.

The win goes to Lady Clara.

It would be lovely. A vindication.

But she was not here for vindication.

She had to think of the long game. If she won now, they would watch her later. She might become mildly interesting. She could not afford to be interesting. Not now.

Although it physically hurt, she laid her cards facedown on the table, withdrawing. Someone snickered. Bram's hands tightened over the back of her chair.

"Perhaps whist might be more to your liking, Lady Clara," Lord Howell said.

Selene played her hand. And won. She tapped the end of her fan flirtatiously on the tip of Lord Howell's nose. "And that's what you get for thinking you are always right."

"I am all apologies."

"Good man."

"I can be even better."

"I look forward to it."

Clara's fingers twitched to take notes, to write down every word of their suggestive banter in the little notebook she kept tucked in her copy of *Four Diocese Sermons*. Instead, she stood up, watching her tokens get claimed. She was fiercely glad Selene had won. Losing to her did not sting. "Good evening."

"Yes," Selene agreed, rising gracefully. "I think that's me done as well."

There was a chorus of protests. "You're not going to give us a chance to win our money back?"

"Certainly not."

Clara held her secret triumph close all the way past the dancers and into the gardens. Torches had been lit in a procession down to the pond, where musicians played a lively tune. Acrobats cartwheeled and somersaulted, wearing very tight spangles. The moon turned the water to silver and silk. Her dress suddenly felt like glittering gossamer instead of plain white satin.

"Gah, pale as a ghost, that one," Lord Whitlow said loudly, with an exaggerated start, when he saw her. "And just as dour."

It was a struggle to hold on to her sense of confidence, but Clara would not relinquish it so easily. She had earned it, even if she had not been able to show the world even a peek at who she really was. Who she could be. And even if she chose to never leave the comforts of her disguise, she deserved the same courtesy as anyone else. Disreputable house party or not.

Lord Whitlow said something to his companion, who laughed, eyes darting toward Clara.

He was still smirking when Bram crossed the grass and then very calmy leaned over and pushed him into the pond. Lord Whitlow went top over teakettle, as Matilda would say.

Someone gasped; someone laughed themselves into a state of hiccups. Someone else snorted.

That was her. The snort of a laugh was definitely her.

She couldn't help it. The expression on Lord Whitlow's face. The resounding splash when he fell in. The affronted departure of the waterfowl currently enjoying the pond—it was all so glorious. Perhaps Clara had not been able to claim a public victory, but she had the image of the viscount choking on water weeds to treasure for the rest of her life.

Bram did not even look over his shoulder to see if the man could swim. She half expected the marquis to send a footman to remove Bram from the premises. Two footmen. Make that three.

But nobody came. Nobody dared.

In fact, it was simply part of the entertainments.

Bram extended his arm to Clara. "Shall we?"

CHAPTER FIFTEEN

THEY LEFT THE raucous entertainments behind for the quiet shadows, and Clara felt her shoulders loosen. "You probably should not have done that," she said. "But thank you all the same."

"I should have done much worse," he said starkly. "You had the winning hand at the table."

She glanced at him. "You saw?" Of course he had—he seemed to see everything. Even her.

"Clever of you not to give yourself away too soon."

And suddenly the victory felt like it was hers again.

Clara abruptly turned left, away from the dower house.

"Where are you going now?" Bram asked, voice taut in the darkness.

"For a walk," she tossed over her shoulder, feeling bold and a little bit reckless.

It felt nice.

"Not alone." Bram glowered at her.

That felt nice too. It shouldn't, but it absolutely did. She wasn't sure what that said about her. Luckily, this was not the time to investigate her own shortcomings. Plenty of time for that later. She had other investigations to see to, after all.

"I can see a garden wall from my bedroom window and a curious little niche that I swear people keep disappearing into. I want to see what it is."

"Are you sure, lass?"

There was something different about his tone. She narrowed her eyes at him. "You know what's down there, don't you?"

"Aye."

"Well, what is it? A garden folly?"

He cleared his throat. "Of a sort."

He was definitely acting strange. Nothing short of a bolt of lightning would prevent her from exploring now. Was his neck turning red? Surely the very collected Captain Thorn did not *blush*?

"That tears it," she declared.

He studied her for one long moment, the gardens stark and moon-tinted behind him. It smelled of incoming rain and spring flowers. He bowed. "After you, Captain."

He had called her *Captain* again, as if they shared a joke between them. She could not think of anyone else who teased her gently, without malice. It might not be the same as *sweetheart* or *darling*, but it *felt* the same to her.

It shouldn't. It *couldn't*.

But it did.

It bounced around inside her head as they crossed the lawn to the stone door set into the side of a garden wall. Ivy choked the old mortar; a fountain trickled cold water like a song. There was a bench on either side of the door and lanterns attached to the wall. It was…pretty. Unassuming.

"Look up."

She followed the lift of his chin. Above the plain door was a carving of a delicate orchid, under the words *Be Bold*.

"It signifies—"

She cut him off, grinning. "I know what it signifies."

A woman's most intimate place. She did not think what lay beyond was for ladies who espoused all things etiquette and decorum.

So much the better.

"I'm going inside."

He raised his eyebrows. "Are you now? Even though it's locked?"

She slipped the ribbon from under her dress. "I think I might have the key."

Understanding flared in his eyes. "Interesting."

The key from the cottage did not fit the lock. But the key that Miss Taunton had left for her "cousin" most certainly did.

The heavy wooden door creaked open. Flickering firelight welcomed them.

She ought to rein in her curiosity, her interest in the symbolic orchid. It was not seemly of Lady Clara. But here in the quiet midnight shadows glittering with rain, with Bram at her side, she suddenly could not bear to pretend.

The rain began to pelt, and they ducked inside.

The interior of the grotto was a stone hallway with arched openings leading into several chambers. Nude statues of Venus and frolicking nymphs and disconcertingly endowed satyrs escorted them by the light of torches. She imagined they were kept well lit during house parties such as this one. There were flowers in stone niches, fresh from the hothouse. It smelled of roses and incense and damp.

Clara wandered through the chambers, noting the raised daises, the beds and padded benches and baskets of ropes. The manacles secured to one wall, the iron lined with velvet. Her cheeks heated and she refused to glance in Bram's direction. Butterflies invaded her belly even as her usual practical self began to take notes for future books.

She was going to be run out of London with the stories currently taking form in her head.

"There's a smile I've never seen," Bram murmured. He sounded very, very composed. Stoic, even.

"Bram?"

"Yes, Clara?"

"Why would Sybil leave me a key to sex caves?"

"I couldn't say," he replied, amusement lacing his voice.

"The marquis's great-grandfather was a member of the Beggar's Benison," Clara said instead, as instructing and bracing as a governess. Miss Vinegar was a hard one to avoid. "I expect that's why no one has made much of a fuss over this grotto. A quirky family thing, as it were."

The Beggar's Benison were a great deal more than quirky; rumors of their antics were infamous. Their full name was the Most Ancient and Most Puissant Order of the Beggar's Benison and Merryland, Anstruther—Merryland being the euphemism for a woman's private flesh. They were said to share lewd songs amid posture girls posing for their pleasure, and to engage in group masturbation.

"Well, he is a marquis," Bram pointed out drily.

"True."

There was no denying that the marquis's title offered him both privilege and protection. He could have the kind of secrets untitled or less-titled men could not. But she did not think they were here, in the grotto. He did not hide its existence beyond parlor tricks, and nor had his father or father's father. It was either a brilliant cover-up or just another peccadillo. A sex club was hardly unusual.

Sex was nothing to be ashamed of, if you asked Clara. Absconding with women, on the other hand, ought to have him hung by his smalls in the town square. Or at Westminster, preferably.

Even a marquis could be brought low. His valet would know more than anyone else, but he was unlikely to talk to her. She would try anyway, but would focus on the maids at the Hall and the women in the village. Spinsters, dowagers, the innkeeper. Someone had to know *something* about the man.

She could have asked the butler.

Considering he was right here. In the sex caves.

With the valet.

"Damn and blast," she muttered.

Bram was already moving, closing his hand over her mouth to silence her even as urged her into a small, curtained niche. It was just large enough to fit them both, her back pressed against his chest, his mouth near her ear.

Before she could react, before she could decide if she wanted to bite his fingers or suck them into her mouth, all options narrowed to one: stay pressed against each other in the darkness.

"The Moon and Stars have arrived." Selene glided into the main alcove, a dozen women trailing her in various states of shocking dishabille: transparent peignoirs, dresses that pushed their bare breasts over the neckline, a man's frock coat tailored to perfection with nothing but silk stockings beneath. There were three men, one rouged, one oiled, and one as perfectly and fashionably attired as any duke.

"You're late," the butler sniffed. It was quite the feat to look so lofty when the valet was licking the spot behind his ear.

"A queen is never late," Selene declared. Her lips were even redder than they had been before, painted so brightly they gleamed even in the torchlight.

"You'll need to be set up and ready much earlier for the Devil's Night," the butler said tersely, even though his cheeks were flushing. "This is just the preamble for a select few gentlemen."

Selene patted his red cheek. "I know, Whiskers."

"That's not my name."

"But it suits you." The valet grinned, pulling on the butler's very neatly trimmed sideburns. The butler's grumble was good-natured after that point.

And then the other gentlemen arrived.

Meanwhile, Clara was still trapped, still aware of every single inch of Bram's body against hers. He was solid muscle and heat, holding her securely but not too tightly, even as she knew there would be no escaping his grip.

It didn't occur to her to want to.

Selene was holding court already, flirting, explaining the rules: words that granted the speaker, guest or *demimonde*, complete autonomy and immediate cessation of any activity, no matter how seemingly innocuous. Curtained niches in the wall for those who preferred to watch privately. Wine, music, food available. Which alcoves catered to which vices and virtues.

And here was Miss Vinegar, secretly lurking uninvited in the sex caves. With Captain Bram Thorn.

And no exit to be had.

CHAPTER SIXTEEN

THERE WAS A certain order of things, wasn't there?

Flirting, kissing—*something* before this kind of incendiary nearness. Long walks in Hyde Park or dancing at Almack's more than twice in one night. Chaperones and lukewarm lemonade on the veranda.

Instead, a grotto filled with incense and writhing bodies, torchlight, and Bram taking up every available breath of air to be had.

But this was not courting, she reminded herself. This was something else entirely.

His hand was still over her mouth, and it awakened a glimmer inside of her. She wasn't offended or scared, though he threatened to overwhelm her with very little effort. She felt safe. Reckless. Miss Vinegar had been well and truly expelled, if only for the moment.

It was enough.

Hadn't she left London for adventure? To explore her own life before it degraded entirely into the excitement of lichen growing on trees? To embrace the Nightingale in a way she could never have before? She would never have the opportunity to do it again. Not like this. Not here. Not with this man.

There were moments for bravery and moments for pride.

This was a moment for wild abandon.

She pressed back slightly against him, gasping when she encountered his hardness stiffening against her. His fingers tightened slightly over her mouth. "You're playing with fire, lass," he murmured.

She had never been the type to play with fire. She was proper, *reserved*.

Not tonight.

Not when he called her *lass* in that way, voice stroking her roughly. No one had ever called her that before. She tucked it away. One day when she was old, she would remember this handsome captain calling her *lass* as though it meant something. It didn't, of course. But that did not diminish it for her.

She pressed harder, grinding over him. It sent liquid heat through her. She could have sworn he growled in her ear.

And she liked it. Very much.

"Clara." A warning threaded through his voice this time, just as delicious. He gripped her hip, digging his fingers softly into her skin. "You don't know what you're doing."

She rubbed against him harder, slower. She knew exactly what she was doing and wanted him to know it too.

He swore.

She felt like a queen. Like the debutante she had never been: glittering, charming, wanton. There were moans on the other side of the curtains, soft groans, whimpers of pleasure. They were like other hands in the dark, touching her. She squirmed, too aware, too conscious.

"Where do you think you're going?" Bram asked quietly, closing his teeth around her earlobe and tugging gently. A little sound formed in her throat. She reached back, desperate to feel him. "Ah, ah," he clicked his tongue. "This might be your game, but the rules are mine."

She whimpered when he held her still.

"Agreed?" he asked.

She nodded, jerkily. As if her body was not her own.

"My rules," he reminded her sternly. "But yours to stop at

any moment. Do you understand?"

She could have wept with the need to have him touch her.

"Answer me."

She nodded again. He was still covering her mouth, gripping her to his body. His length thickened at the top of her buttocks, nudging against her. And then his lips were on the side of her throat, brushing up and down, softly, so softly. A lick, a tease. A scrape of teeth that sent decadent shivers bolting down her spine.

He lifted the hem of her gown, his ragged breath in her ear, a counterpoint to the soft moans escalating throughout the grotto. He dragged his fingertips up her leg, along her knee, up her thigh. She quivered with anticipation, with a want that clawed through her, urging her to reach back again. He pinned her ruthlessly, fingers pausing at the crease of her thigh. "What did I say?"

She whimpered again but relented.

"You're going to be so quiet for me, aren't you?" he asked. "So *good*."

He slid between her folds, sliding back and forth, inked knuckles wet with her body's response before he eased a finger inside of her. He groaned as if he were the one being stroked, and it only made the heat rise more sharply inside of her. He built a rhythm, thrusting deeply, slowly, circling her nub, trusting harder. Another circle, a flick, a press of his thumb. She moved against him, seeking, reaching, desperate.

"Take it," he said roughly. "It's yours—*take it.*"

She shattered.

There was no Miss Vinegar. No Lady Clara. No spinster or wallflower. Not even the Nightingale.

Only *Clara*.

Pleasure was sharp, a kiss with teeth. A bite. And all the sweeter for it.

She went limp against him, and he smiled into her hair, releasing the hem of her gown.

It had taken Clara barely a few days out of London to succumb to ruination.

It was shameful. Delightful. Not remotely sustainable.

But that was a problem for tomorrow. Next week. It hardly mattered—she would not let her worries and her wishes taint a perfectly decadent evening.

THAT WAS WHY it took her a long, disorienting moment the next morning when she found the note under her door.

I know what you do. Five thousand pounds or the world will know it too.

She froze. Had someone seen her last night? Bram had covered her with his coat when they snuck out. No one had paid the least bit of attention to them. He hadn't said a word as they crept across the cold lawn and back to the Dower House. No one could have overheard a snippet of conversation and recognized them. Even when he walked her to her bedroom door, he did not say a single word. His eyes glittered fiercely before he took his leave. After searching her room, of course, to ascertain that it was safe.

Nightingale, she reminded herself. This was about her books. Nothing else.

Though she was a little bit proud of herself that she now had *two* scandalous dealings that might lead to blackmail.

It was not enough to smother the fear that followed. She lived alone on the small annuity granted to her by her father's estate. The new earl who had succeeded him, a cousin who was decent enough but had no interest in anything outside of horses, would not increase her allowance. And he would not shield her if word got out of what she secretly did for a living. She would lose her income, her reputation. Her house. Everything.

She knew all too well what could happen to women in London.

She had thought she would get a reprieve by leaving. But had the blackmailer followed her? Was he here even now? A tremor of dread made her feel queasy. She crumpled up the note, considered tossing it onto the fire, and tucked it into her cuff instead. She might need to investigate them further, inspect the handwriting again.

She did not have five thousand pounds. It was an exorbitant amount. A *desperate* amount.

She would investigate the marquis. Then her own problems.

First, breakfast. It was not much of a plan, admittedly, but it was better than sitting in her room and giving in to the rising panic. Anything was better than that.

She'd clearly forgotten what it was like to have breakfast with a roomful of bored and hungover aristocrats. More fool her.

The breakfast room dripped gold and crystal, which, if the squinting was anything to go by, was not ideal the morning after overindulging. Spoons clinked against cups, the strong scent of coffee and tea mingling. Miss Abernathy looked like she might weep if the footman took any longer bringing her a cup. She nearly took off one of his fingers when he finally moved to set the coffee in front of her, and she did not look the least bit sorry over it.

"Did you hear?" someone murmured. "There is a new Nightingale chapbook on sale this week. I am sorry to miss it. That odd little bookstore always reserves a copy for me."

Clara paused at the sideboard, then went back to scooping eggs onto her plate. She added an extra pastry to give herself time to compose her expression. Especially when she could not stop her mind from wandering back to the dark niche under the garden wall where Bram had stroked her to pleasure.

Her. Lady Clara Prescott, spinster and wallflower.

When she turned around, she was as placid as a morning pond. And just as interesting.

"Do try to keep your morning sermon to yourself," a lady sniffed when Clara sat down. "Not that I expect you even know who the Nightingale is." No less than four gentlemen smirked in response.

As Clara had no intention of talking to her at all, never mind pontificating, she did not reply. Although she was very, very tempted to memorize the longest, stuffiest passage from the oldest, stuffiest book in the house library for the next morning's meal. Something with lepers. Possibly boils.

"The moon goddess herself," Lord Howell sang out when Selene joined them. She wore a dark green dress, very plain but with a neckline that hinted at far more interesting pleasures. The other women from her house of ill repute did not join her. That *would* have been beyond the pale. Clara was fairly certain Selene was only welcomed because she had the confidence and the audacity to assume she would be. To demand it.

Clara...not exactly.

"The Nightingale," Selene muttered, taking the seat next to Clara in a cloud of perfume bright with notes of fruit. Not at all the sultry scent one might have expected.

"Do you know her?" Clara asked carefully.

"I only know her books, like everyone else. And the fact that she has caused me no end of trouble."

"How so?"

"Bodies do not quite bend in the way she assumes, and yet no one will believe us, marching around the henhouse waving her chapbooks around."

Clara honestly did not know what to say to that.

Thank you? I'm sorry?

What she *wanted* to say was: *How do they bend, then? Which parts did I get wrong? May I visit you just once? Because I have a thousand follow-up questions.*

She couldn't say any of that, of course. Instead, she made some vague noise of commiseration.

"Tell me, how is it a courtesan is better received than an earl's daughter?" Selene said, perfectly unfazed with all of the glances being thrown her way, covert and obvious, complimentary and judgmental. As if she had not spent the night cavorting in the grotto with several of the gentlemen here.

As if Clara had not done the same.

"You are very beautiful and witty." Clara spread butter on her toast very evenly. "The *ton* forgives most foibles if you are pretty enough. Or rich enough."

"Pish."

Clara put her knife down, angling it precisely. "It's not flattery," she said. "Well, not *only* flattery. It's the truth."

Selene looked at her over the rim of her teacup. "If you wore bright blue or emerald green instead of that terrible muddy gray, and you allowed me to soften your hair, you could have them vying for your attention."

"That sounds dreadful." Clara wrinkled her nose. "No, thank you." She might not enjoy being overlooked and mocked, but she did not think she would enjoy being the center of attention either. Especially not here, where she had covert business to see to.

Not to mention, she might even now be sharing a pot of tea with her blackmailer.

Was it Lord Howell? Lord Whitlow? Lady Falstaff?

There were dozens of guests. And it all seemed too implausible. More likely her blackmailer had hired someone to deliver the note: a footman, a lady's maid, the baker's son from the village delivering sticky buns shaped like nymphs for teatime. As always, the list of possibilities was endless.

She suddenly felt a little queasy and very carefully set down her forkful of potatoes.

ACROSS THE TABLE, Bram frowned.

Clara was up to something.

She was uneasy, but not in the way social events usually made her uneasy. He knew the difference at a glance. She looked nervous. Guilty.

He hoped like hell it had nothing to do with the previous night's activities. Never in a million years would he have thought he would be trapped in a grotto with Lady Clara Prescott. That she would let him touch that soft, delicate skin. That her muffled whimpers would be for him alone.

Best not think on it. Growing hard at the breakfast table was not done on any level of society. And it wasn't the perfumed hothouse flowers descended from earls and dukes, nor the sultry Selene, who affected him this way. It was the quiet, moon-haired spinster with a devil's own heart.

Her secret mischief only made her all the harder to resist.

The discomfort as she sipped her tea from a cup painted with orchids made him want to smash the table into tiny pieces. Was she scared? Nervous of him? The thought made his chest feel like it might collapse, the same dreadful pressure that being indoors for too long caused him. He needed the open sky, the relentless battering of the wind. Clara.

The more properly she dressed, the primmer her expression, the more he wanted to undo her. To make her forget every rule of decorum the way she had in his arms last night, however briefly. She was bright as the full moon in the night sky, and how no one else seemed to notice was beyond him.

He should probably apologize.

But he wasn't the least bit sorry. In fact, it had only made him hungrier for her. Ravenous.

But social norms dictated it.

Mulishly, he did not want to apologize for giving her pleasure, for watching her take it wholeheartedly.

More importantly, he wanted to know why she kept glancing around, then fiddling with a piece of paper hiding under the cuff of her sleeve.

CHAPTER SEVENTEEN

THEY HAD A key that unlocked a door to a grotto of disrepute, and other keys with nothing to unlock.

It was maddening.

Nothing fit any lock in the dining room. Nor the library. Nor the dower house. It could literally be anywhere else. Was it for a door, a cabinet, a box? A garden shed? The marquis's bedroom?

Perhaps Clara was not cut out to investigate misdeeds and bring bad men to justice, after all.

She hurried up the main stairs. The other guests had dispersed to play billiards and walk through the village, as the sun was warm today, coaxing more tulips and bluebells out of the ground. Clara wondered if anyone would think to buy Granny Mab naughty-looking pastries.

After last night, those pastries suddenly made a lot more sense.

Which meant the grotto was hardly a secret. So why, then, had Sybil left a key?

"I know you weren't disobeying me and wandering off alone," Bram said suddenly from behind her, lethally calm.

She yelped, loudly enough to put her goose army to shame. He was on the landing behind her, arms crossed and watching her with a single raised eyebrow. She would have raised one right back if she knew how to. "Must you lurk?" she asked.

"Must you?"

"I wasn't lurking! I was walking," she said. "Anyway, I already told you I'm invisible."

"I see you very clearly, Lady Clara."

What did that mean? Anything? Should she ask? Ignore it?

If she did ask, would they have to talk about last night? Would she have to listen to him tell her that it was just a fleeting moment, more to do with the atmosphere than with her? Or worse, that his honor required some sort of forced relationship between them? That he regretted it? She would rather it meant nothing at all.

Or even worse yet, would he say nothing? Because she was small and pale and they were in a place where everything and everyone glittered?

Back to the task at hand. Safer for her heart.

Pride. She'd meant pride, of course.

"Where are you going?"

Right round the maypole if she continued to chase her thoughts in this fruitless manner. Better to chase a missing chaperone and a key with no lock. "I was going to the nursery."

"Alone?" His tone was so stern and disapproving, she considered saluting.

"With you, clearly."

He grumbled under his breath as he stalked after her. "Why are we here?" he asked when they stepped onto the nursery floor. "There have been no children in this house for some time."

"I know," she said, noting the wooden rocking horse in the corner, the bed, and the rest of the furniture draped in white cloths. Dust motes danced lazily in the air, and light streamed through the narrow windows. There was a chalkboard hanging on one wall still bearing a drawing of a hedgehog with a sword. He was fighting a mighty dragon who appeared to be more interested in his cup of tea. He wore spectacles.

Beyond that was a sitting room much better suited for a debutante. It was simple, perhaps hastily done, but pretty. Mint-green chairs, lace curtains, scrolled tables. A chest that was at least two hundred years old but recently painted with doves. Black, naturally.

Clara went straight for it. "I found out from my lady's maid that this was where Sybil and Heloise actually stayed."

"Why didn't you tell me?"

"We were otherwise occupied." She meant with the party, not the bit where he lifted her skirts in his big, tattooed hands and she writhed against him helplessly. She'd even dreamed of it a few hours later. She cleared her throat. "Isn't it curious that I was told when we arrived that their rooms were in the family wing?"

No wonder they had felt so soulless and smelled of lemon polish, like guest rooms without occupants.

She opened the chest, peering inside. Drawing pencils, water-color paints, a deck of cards, a basket of half-finished needlepoint. Nothing that locked, nothing that explained the mysteries piling up around them. She dropped the lid, disgruntled.

Bram prowled through the rooms, much like she imagined he would have prowled the deck of a ship, the wind in his face, his curls tangling at his brow. How many storms had he sailed into? How many battles had he faced, cannons and swords and muskets? He had so many scars, many far too long to be the result of those dreaded splinters. She shivered.

"Are you spooked?" Bram asked, faintly amused.

"By an empty nursery?" she shot back. "Hardly." It would be ridiculous to tell him she worried about him, the *him* of two years ago, five years ago. Phantom battles. Did the war haunt him as it haunted so many others?

She turned her attention to the shelves, still holding old books on mathematics and Latin and the lives of the great painters of the Renaissance. Not to mention stodgy old poetry no one bothered with anymore. Sybil had left no clues there.

Bram looked at the books in her hand, around the room again. "My sisters never had a governess. Is this what it was like for you?"

"A little," she replied. She'd had a nursemaid, a governess, and her mother. Rules and more rules. And then her father, scrambling to undo them all whenever he could, for his amusement. It was not a comfortable house. "How many sisters do you have?" she asked, instantly consumed with curiosity.

"Two, both younger than me. My father tutored them."

"And you?"

"I went to the naval academy."

"Was your father also in the navy?"

"No, but my grandfather was."

"Your youngest sister's name was Marielle, wasn't it?"

"Yes. She had that spot of trouble while I was away. Priya stepped in."

"And that's why you help the Spinsters."

"Partly."

She could think of at least a hundred more questions she wanted to ask him. She had not met his sister, as she was not part of the Society at the time. But if she asked, he would ask questions of his own.

The blackmail note she had shoved in her sleeve itched accusatorily.

She crossed to the main bedroom, which had to belong to Heloise, with its canopied bed, dressing table, cheval glass. The water pitcher and bowl were painted with a red dove. Sybil had trusted Heloise.

Little clues everywhere, and still Clara could not see the whole picture.

She checked under the bed and found a hatbox containing love letters, a gold bracelet, and three Nightingale books. The small, attached bedroom would have belonged to a nursemaid and then to a governess as the children grew older. It had a bed, a chair, and a windowsill cluttered with a collection of shiny river pebbles under a sloped ceiling.

"Nothing," Bram announced from the doorway. "You?"

"More doves—nothing clear, though." Had Sybil realized she

would have to flee soon and was not sure who would follow her and how? Why the keys and the doves and the riddles?

But Clara also knew something about hiding secrets, both metaphorically and physically. She never kept her manuscripts under her mattress or rolled up in the flour canister. If one was serious, one had to be cleverer than that.

And Sybil was very clever. She would not hide a key near the item it unlocked. Assuming she had not just sent Clara random keys that could have opened anything from the privy to the tea caddy.

Chaperones, like governesses, occupied a kind of in-between space. Not servant enough to eat in the servants' hall, not high enough in the instep to eat with the family. They moved from nursery to schoolroom to bedroom with very little access to the rest of the house. Not that that would stop Sybil. Very little stopped Sybil: not storms or fire, not the Thames or the Prince of Wales himself.

Clara was beginning to get nervous again.

"What are you looking for?" Bram asked in that honey-rough voice of his.

"I'm not sure," she replied, still floating from room to room, corner to corner. "But she must have hidden something here as well. Although if it's another key, I don't see how that will help."

"Right under everyone's noses?"

"She might not have had enough time for anything else. She might have stopped in the village while she was running. It was luck for us that Granny Mab spotted her." Or more likely, Sybil had *chosen* Granny Mab to spot her. Just in case.

Clara followed the doves because it was all she could think to do in the moment. There were three red doves and the rest were black, all facing in the same direction. From the classroom, the chest, the wall. All facing toward the chaise longue.

And the blue dove above it, crowning the window just above the curtain frippery.

It matched the others, down to the little spiral at the end of its talon. Sybil's personal mark.

And it was the same blue, incidentally, as the velvet coats the marquis preferred.

Bram followed her gaze. "You'd have done well in a bird's nest, love, with those sharp eyes."

She would not be distracted by the flush of pleasure at his praise.

Clara went to the window and lifted the glass. A clean breeze snuck past her, rustling the curtains. The hills were a vibrant green, crossed with gray stone walls and towering oak trees. Below, gardens bursting into color, a wandering guest here and there, none looking up.

She leaned out and found she was considerably higher up than that Mayfair mansion was, and sincerely hoped she would not have to crawl out. When she inched forward, Bram was very suddenly at her side. "Don't even think about it," he said between his teeth.

She looked up, to the right, to the left. It was mostly thick, trailing ivy clinging to the white stone. But just *there*, tucked into the green tangle—the glint of brass.

"I have something!" she squeaked, excited.

She twisted and stretched. Bram immediately clapped his hands around her waist, securing her. "Almost have it..." She stretched a little further, her neck muscles stinging. Her knuckles scraped the stone. She was going to have the hands of a bruiser. All she needed was her own tattoo. *Prim* across one hand. The *ton* would faint en masse in shock.

"Are you giggling again?"

"Absolutely not."

She finally felt the object, which seemed to be a smallish box. She probably would not drop it on the head of an unsuspecting guest below. Probably.

"You are definitely giggling."

She grabbed hold and pulled it loose, ducking back inside. Bram did not release her straightaway. His eyes were hard, hot.

Or cold? She could not tell. Her body only knew that he was so close, and focused on her again.

Her brain knew it must be for the investigation.

Her body was not listening to her brain. In fact, it had shouted nasty names and slammed the proverbial door shut. It took every bit of her self-control not to press against his warm, solid heft. To bite his lower lip, just once. To see what he would do. What *she* would do.

But alas, a Spinster must Spinster.

"It's a box," she blurted out, holding it up.

It was not much bigger than her hand, plain, dark wood with brass hinges. Nothing particular about it all. Except for its location. Clara met Bram's blue eyes, stunned. "We actually found something."

Take that, rules of etiquette and pouring more tea than anyone could reasonably drink—she was a proper Spinster now.

Her thighs were still far more interested in Bram's proximity.

She took a key from where it dangled down the front of her stays on a thin chain. It was still warm from her body heat when she slid it into the lock.

It fit.

A turn, a satisfying click.

She lifted the lid.

The words she used were not fit for even the filthiest Nightingale story. Bram's eyebrows lifted. "Not a captain after all with that mouth, but a pirate. Suits you better."

She decided she could sway just a little closer to him. He was so big and he smelled so good, always like rain and lime candies, and for some reason he knew the perfect things to say.

One small problem remained.

Another blasted key.

Anticipation and excitement slammed into each other and broke apart, a shipwreck on the rocks. She visibly deflated. Bram swore. Clara held the box upside down, shaking it. Nothing fell out to helpfully solve the mystery. "Bollocks."

Bram just shook his head, and she could have sworn he was hiding a smile.

Meanwhile, she was trying—unsuccessfully, it had to be said—not to sulk.

"Sybil is," Clara said, very calmly for a pirate, "I'm sorry to say, beginning to vex me. We clearly need a more practical way of sending messages."

"I have no doubt you can sort that out."

Wait.

"This has a false bottom," she said softly.

CHAPTER EIGHTEEN

B RAM SUDDENLY HAD a dagger in his hand. She had no idea where he had been hiding it. Or why it made him even more attractive. Why she couldn't stop staring at the tendons in his wrist, the deft strength of his fingers, the faded rope burns. "Give it here."

He fit the tip of the blade into the edge and pried the side loose. The bottom popped up, normally held aloft with wine corks in each corner and a wire lever. "No more bloody puzzles."

On the true bottom of the box lay a letter, sealed with wax with a blue dove painted over the seal.

Footsteps sounded up the narrow stairs, across the playroom. Clara grabbed Bram's arm without thinking. If they were discovered, they would lose their advantage. She was supposed to be invisible.

"Do you trust me?" Bram whispered.

She nodded mutely, slipping the letter down the front of her stays, along with the new key.

It was all he needed. A nod of her head and he muscled her toward the desk, lifting her onto it. Her dress rode up to her knees, showing her silk stockings and the little red ribbons. He stared at them before finally looking back up at her, eyes flaring. "Have you been wearing those under your dress the whole time?"

She nodded again.

His mouth closed over her in a kiss that swept through her like a tempest, like he was pushed to his limits. One big hand closed around her knee, the other tangled in her hair, all while he continued to suck at her lower lip, lick into her mouth, drag his teeth under her jaw. She melted—her bones simply melted away as heat rushed through her, pulling at her belly and lower. She widened her thighs so he could press even closer, the length of him against her softest, most intimate place. She whimpered, could not help herself. His thumb stroked up past her red ribbons, touching her bare thigh.

She kissed him back just as hungrily, until he groaned, pushing against her, grinding up until she whimpered again. She needed more. All of it. He kissed her throat, his mouth hot and clever, a pulse answering in her breasts, in her quim. She rubbed against him, helplessly chasing that delicious friction, the groan rumbling in his throat.

"Just what do you think—" The intruder cut himself off.

Bram turned his head, but only slightly. His pupils were wide, darkening his eyes. Her skin prickled from the scratch of his beard. He was still fitted against her, arms wrapped around her, her legs dangling on either side of him.

"Is there a problem?" he demanded of the footman, one of the ones who looked too large and angry to be a footman.

"No one's allowed up here," the footman said, scowling.

"It's a house party, mate," Bram said easily. "And a Devil's Night. Can't blame me."

The footman snorted. "Try the gate at the back of the garden."

He left, but his footsteps stopped on the stairs. He was not going to go anywhere until they had. Never mind—they had what they needed, with no one the wiser.

Bram stepped back. She smoothed her dress down, the white so stark against the black of his trousers. "All right, pirate?" he asked quietly.

She nodded, forcing herself to smile briskly. "Of course."

He narrowed his eyes. "Should I apologize?" he asked.

She would crumble away into humiliated ashes if he dared. "Certainly not."

He had kissed her to save them from discovery. Not because he could not stop replaying their moment in the caves in his head the way she did. Constantly. So that it was difficult to think of anything else.

Once again, she had to remind herself that he touched her out of necessity. Not desire. After all, any man might desire a woman in a grotto devoted to orgies. Even someone like her. And she already knew he was set on being a protector. It was just in his nature.

"That was close," she murmured. She moved to hop down, to remember who she was.

His hand remained on her knee, gripping tight. He stayed where he was, his eyes fierce and calculating. "Clara, have you really been wearing those under your dresses this whole time?"

"Yes."

He stepped back very carefully, as if she was the dangerous one. He ran a hand over his jaw. "I've survived hurricanes and cannon fire and bloody Napoleon. But I don't think I'll survive you."

Suddenly, she felt rather better about the whole thing.

The footman was indeed waiting on the landing, not even pretending to be occupied with some other chore. Clara kept her gaze lowered—she did not want him to remember her.

"My apologies," Bram said, without an ounce of actual apology in his voice. "Won't happen again."

Clara refused to acknowledge that depressing thought. Not while she was still damp and slick under her dress, aching for his fingers and his tongue.

Not to mention smuggling a letter and another mysterious key.

Bram and Clara did not speak the entire journey down the stairs, through the conservatory and the garden and all the way back to the dower house. The footman abandoned them somewhere on the second landing, but Clara swore she could feel him watching them through the window.

The dower house was empty, save for a new tray of fresh rolls and strawberry jam from Mrs. Meadows and an assortment of mint teas from the garden. Clara broke the wax seal off the letter before she had gotten more than two steps inside.

Dear Cousin,

If you are reading this, it does not bode well for me. But felicitations on finding this letter at all. I left as many clues as I could, but necessity called for me to leave many more that led nowhere. I have tried to run away with Heloise, as you must have gathered for yourself, but I fear the marquis is on our trail. I do not know if we will make it. He is even worse than we feared. Heloise is not the first to be stolen by him and kept locked away, all for the sake of keeping her considerable inheritance and dowry under his purview. I pray you ask about a Miss Blanche Yarwood, daughter of a wool merchant from Cardiff, and Lady Rosalinde Fairfax from Ireland. I have proof that not only did the marquis abduct them and steal their fortunes, but he is also behind the demise of their previous guardians to that end. I am afraid I have hidden the evidence elsewhere and cannot tell you where, though I have every confidence you will find it in time. I cannot risk it, lest he finds this first. It is our only leverage at present. He searches for us even now.

Be safe and be very, very careful. Yours, S.T.

"Worse and worse." Clara set the letter down. "Abduction, theft, murder. How are we going to find Sybil if we can't even find the evidence that she has hidden away?"

"We'll manage."

"Why would he even do all of this? He has all of those estates and houses. He has more money than Prinny himself."

"But like Prinny, he might be in debt up to his eyeballs," Bram pointed out. "It's not uncommon."

"Perhaps that's why he's hosting the Devil's Night?"

"Perhaps."

"Poor Sybil. She is relying on us, and all we have is a key that leads to a grotto anyone can get into this week, and a key that opens a box to another key that opens we don't know what."

"She has leverage," Bram reminded her when her shoulders dropped. "She will be fine."

"For how long?"

"Long enough," he replied grimly.

CHAPTER NINETEEN

CLARA SPENT THE rest of the afternoon in the grand library, pretending to read wholesome tracts on morals and decorum. In fact, she was combing through the shelves looking for any more letters from Blanche, any mention of Rosalinde. Anything that might give her a better idea of the marquis and Eastbourne Hall.

What she really needed was better technical drawings. Something by an artist with a keen eye for detail. Mentions of a dungeon. Or a locked tower.

She searched for sketches from the first marquis who built the house in the late sixteenth century, taking note of areas that might be forgotten or abandoned, such as old turrets, the ruins of the family chapel, any place where Sybil might have hidden evidence.

Or, conversely, where the marquis might have hidden Sybil.

And why the secret passageway led to what appeared to be a parlor from some time ago.

Too many questions.

So few answers.

By the time the sun set, the last thing Clara wanted was to endure another night of dancing and cards and flirting. She desperately wanted to stay in her room and memorize more rules of the card games she had never played before for the Devil's

Night, just in case.

But even a spinster had to make an appearance.

The drawing rooms thrummed with a different kind of energy. Sharp, watchful. Dangerous.

Clara soon found out that while she was in the library, the Devil himself had arrived.

He sat in a burgundy leather chair with gilded lion's-paw feet. Two men stood at his side, large, hawk-eyed. Body men. They did not even try to pretend otherwise. There was no disguising them as footmen, or friends. And Clara knew without being told that they were more effective then the marquis's footmen.

The party had been all songbirds and swans, and now the eagles and the hawks were flying low. The Devil was just as handsome as she might have expected, with dark hair, dark eyes, a sinful curve to his lips. A cold knowing in his eye, as if nothing escaped his attention. As if he searched for something. And did not find it.

The marquis held court in the opposite corner, all flash and charm. The diamonds on his cravat pin caught the light, just as he did, holding attention in a different manner, his blue coat the color of bluebird feathers. Whereas the Devil had a certain sinister air, it was the marquis who made her uneasy.

Bram leaned against the gold damask wallpaper, their opposite, and yet holding every bit as much interest. Clara saw it in the way the guests circled, constantly glancing between them all, most without even realizing it. He caught her gaze, held it. His stern, uncompromising expression did not change, and yet she felt the difference. She felt it in her thighs and in the sudden tightening of her nipples.

And then the energy changed.

Suddenly. Without warning.

There were too many guests for her to see exactly what was happening, but one moment it was all the clinking of wine glasses and candlelight, and then a figure pushed through the crowd. Someone shouted. A goblet fell, smashing to pieces.

A dagger flashed, held high.

Impossible to see what happened next, as Clara was suddenly thrown to the parquet floor, Bram's body shielding hers completely. His eyes were fierce, savage. She caught her breath under the weight of him.

"Are you all right?" he demanded. "Clara, are you hurt?"

"I'm fine," she squeaked.

Cacophony erupted, but it was the milling of those songbirds pecking at seeds, fluttering bright feathers. He tracked them for a moment before helping her up. The marquis wiped wine off his blue coat, like spilled blood. His hands were shaking.

"Chin up, Eastbourne." Devil laughed coldly from the melee. "It's not a Devil's Night until someone attempts a murder."

That someone was already crashing through a window left open to help cool the heated, perfumed air. "Red hair," Bram said. "Clara, can you run?"

She grabbed the skirts of her boring dress and shot his own words back at him from the first time they had chased a man with red hair who was keen on knives.

"Keep up, Captain Thorn."

It was much easier to find a horse this time.

The marquis had extensive stables, a great number of horses, and a veritable army to care for them. In fact, they had already seen to a horse for a man with red hair who was staying only long enough to deliver a message.

Perhaps he had nothing to do with Sybil, but he clearly had something to do with the event, Devil, and, therefore, possibly the marquis. Enough to try to kill him, which was an immediate hanging offense.

And there was that minor detail where he had tried to stab Bram.

It was providential that he was clearly not very good at stabbing. And murdering.

Less providential that it was raining again.

But then, it was March in England, and that was no very great surprise. Bram stripped off his coat as they ran for the stables and bundled Clara into it before helping her up into the saddle. Every part of him screamed at her to stay behind. But he knew she wouldn't. And the safety of the Hall had not markedly improved with the removal of a single man with a dagger. "You're safer with me," he muttered.

But not safe enough.

The light flashing off that dagger, the shocked screams, all within feet of Clara, was enough to make him feel sick. Furious. He was supposed to protect her.

And yes, the man hadn't been there for her, and even the bloody marquis was taken by surprise, though he had burly footmen at his disposal. None of that mattered. There had been violence entirely too close to Lady Clara Prescott. Again.

Bram liked it better when she pasted up posters in ladies' retiring rooms or delivered messages to Priya in her plain little reticule. At least she was safe then. But it didn't take a genius to know she hated being safe all of the time. A blind man could see it.

The clouds thickened, stealing every bit of the dying light that struggled to pierce them. The world was gray and shadowy and wet, and it was still better than the warm, perfumed drawing room. Her nose was cold, her dress little shield to the elements. And he knew she preferred it. Her grin told him everything he needed to know, as did the steely expression of determination. He would have to tie her up to keep her away from any of this.

Unbidden, the image of Clara wearing nothing but those red silk ribbons around her wrists, securing her to his bedposts, flashed though his mind.

Those damn red ribbons had been driving him mad since he'd seen them secured around her thighs in the attic. He had wanted to undo them with his teeth. To lick at the faint marks they left behind on her pale skin. Wanted, wanted, *wanted*.

Even now, riding through the cold spring rain, soaked through, his body responded to the image. A little wet weather meant nothing. Clara meant everything.

"You madwoman," Bram called from his horse as rain dripped off her nose. "How many times do I need to tell you that you're not supposed to be enjoying this?"

She only clung tighter to the reins and laughed. She'd have made a hell of a sailor. She was a better rider than he would ever be. He was passable, but he'd spent too many years on a ship. The rolling of the waves was second nature to him, not this. And he was not particularly young anymore.

The man with red hair did not stop in the village but continued on toward Fitcher, as Bram had earlier tracked from the ruined tower. They caught sight of him once but could not quite catch up. It was galling.

The rain intensified as they passed through the medieval city gates, the ground turning to mud under the horses' hooves. Bram questioned the night porter, who pointed down the street to the left where a man had just arrived, riding hard. The buildings jutted out over the street, affording a small respite from the rain, but not for long. The storm was only getting worse. They passed a haberdashery, a shop that sold parasols, another specializing in snuff blends. The locals were already inside, sensibly dry. He wanted Clara by a fire, drinking something to warm her up.

Bram glared through the rain. A dog ran by with a stolen boot in his mouth. A window slammed shut above them. Laughter and gold light spilled from a nearby house. He noted them all but spent no more than a moment on each. They weren't his quarry, and they weren't a threat to Clara, and so they were nothing.

"There," he said with grim satisfaction. Clara followed the jut of his chin toward the courtyard at the end of the street, leading to an inn that backed the river.

"The Starchy Governess," she said above the sound of water hitting rooftop and cobblestones and shop signs. "If Sybil came this way, she definitely went in there. That can't be a coincidence."

He didn't ask how she knew—the Spinsters had strange ways of communicating. If she said it mattered, then it mattered. And beyond the creaking inn sign was the brown horse with white hocks that they had been following for half an hour. A stable boy was leading her into the stables.

They'd found the blighter.

At the inn Sybil would have chosen.

He didn't believe in coincidences. Sailors were too superstitious for that.

"You're waiting here." He couldn't help it. It was a command, ripped from years of shouting orders but also from the fear rooting in his very soul.

Clara slid out of the saddle, right into a dirty puddle. His fists clenched. "Don't be ridiculous," she said, exactly as he'd known she would. "I am going through the front door."

"The hell you are."

"I am going through the front door," she repeated, drenched and pale, her teeth chattering slightly. Every shiver may as well have been a dagger right through his throat. "And what's more, I am going to make a great big fuss about it."

He pushed his sodden hair back. "Clara. I'm begging you."

She was already darting away. "He barely had a lead on us. He's still trying to rent a room, I'd bet my books on it. I'll walk in; he will panic and run for the back door. Where *you'll* be waiting."

It wasn't a bad plan. Except for one glaring fault.

"And if he comes at you instead? With that knife?"

She tossed him a smile over her shoulder. *A smile.*

"Let's find out, shall we?"

She was clearly every bit the madwoman Bram had accused her of being. This was a *terrible* plan.

But it was hers. And it was too late now.

SHE PUSHED INTO the inn, the warmth and the cheerful clatter momentarily disorienting. Two men shouted over a game of dice; another played a fiddle in the corner. Women laughed over pints of ale. A cat wound around Clara's feet before darting away behind the bar toward the kitchen. The innkeeper stood at that bar, piling glasses onto the tray of a barmaid who could only be his daughter, all while accepting coin from a man dripping a puddle on the wooden floors smoothed by decades of boots.

A red-haired man.

He turned at the opening of the front door, saw Clara, and gaped.

Properly gaped.

And not just because she was wearing a man's frock coat several sizes too large for her over a ruined, wet ball gown. He recognized her.

He turned and ran, shoving through the patrons to get to the back door.

"Got you," she said with more smugness than was genteel.

He jostled the barmaid, who was far too experienced to let the tray tilt. Not a drop was spilled, but she yelled a curse that could have withered the fur off a donkey's backside. The innkeeper frowned, then glanced at Clara. "Here now, come in and get dry, lass."

"Thank you," she smiled, approaching him. She tried not to feel anxious about so many people watching her. She wasn't used to it.

"Are you alone, then? Caught in the storm?"

"No, my…husband is seeing to the horses. But yes, the storm caught us out a bit." She pushed her heavy, wet hair off her neck where it was slipping free of its pins as the word *husband* reverberated on her tongue. A necessary lie, but one she was still glad Bram had not heard her make. He'd think her silly, smitten. And she was. "I wasn't expecting it."

"Don't get a lot of fine ladies in here, don't mind saying." The innkeeper's smile was friendly, and his bald head gleamed in the light of the tallow candles. He was short and very wide. His warm eyes flickered over her shoulder, turned to iron. "Off with ye, Albert."

"But she's pretty."

"I'll thump you, see if I won't."

"Never mind that," his daughter broke in. She had coal-black curls caught in a bandeau. "I'll tell your wife, you great big lout."

Albert slunk away, grumbling.

"I'm Bess," she said to Clara. "Why don't you come wait in the back parlor? They're good lads, mostly, but they'll pester you, I think. You look like a wee angel."

Clara would have married Bess right then and there if she'd asked.

"Da, give us a whiskey for the girl," Bess said. "She's turning blue."

"Aye, and your sister's making her famous mutton stew. I'll send over a bowl."

"Thank you, I—" Clara did not have time to finish her sentence. Bess was already bustling her to the back door, through a curtain and into a small, private parlor with a roaring fire and ceramic ducks on the mantel. Clara sat down, grateful for the warmth. Bram's coat was heavy with rain, but she was still reluctant to part with it. It smelled like him: water and wood smoke and lime candies. She draped it near the fire for him.

Bess returned, delivering a whiskey, a tea tray, and a plate of hard cheese and fresh, dark bread. It was not in the shape of a man's buttocks, regrettably. Montragroux had definitively cornered that particular market.

Within minutes, Bram made his own delivery: a sopping wet, yelping gentleman, squirming like a trout in the talons of an eagle.

Clara leaned back in her wobbly chair and smiled. "What took you so long?"

Chapter Twenty

B RAM LOOKED LIKED something out of one of her own stories. The hero charging in out of the rain, grim-faced, fiery-eyed. If she'd been writing it, there would have been no would-be assassin intruding. Nor that wet linen shirt, however nicely it molded to his chest muscles. There would be no shirt at all.

She wondered if Bram would recognize himself if she snuck him into a chapbook. Not that he read them. Not that she was guaranteed another book, if her blackmailer continued to be a pest.

One catastrophe at a time.

"He bolted, just like you said he would," Bram said, knocking her out of her thoughts. "Luckily, he's as shite at running as he is at stabbing."

"You came out of nowhere!" the man protested, then yelped when Bram shook him, still gripping the back of his collar.

"You tried to kill me."

"I thought you were sent by the marquis!"

Bram slammed him up against the wall, rattling the ceramic ducks and knocking a drawing of a wide-eyed lamb sideways. "And you put that lady in danger," he ground out. There was murder written all over his face. "You're going to tell us everything you know or I'm going to break several of your bones. Starting with your kneecap."

"Red dove!" the man gasped, clearly believing Bram's willingness to follow through on his threats. He was sweating under the rainwater.

Bram frowned. "I haven't even hit you yet—you can't be addled already."

"Stop," Clara said.

"He tried to stab someone in front of you. Twice."

"But he didn't try to stab *me*." She felt warmth in her chest from his outrage. Over *her*. Miss Vinegar. "But he did try to stab *you*, so feel free to shake him around a little, but don't hurt him *too* much. Yet."

"Yet?"

"Red dove means he's telling the truth," she explained. "Between Spinsters. Or he will be as soon as he tells us anything of value. Isn't that right, Mr.…?"

"Y-yes," the man said. "Martin. Martin Townsend."

Bram sighed, jaw clenching, before dropping him.

Martin half-slid down the wall. "You're the size of a bloody bear."

Clara narrowed her eyes in case he had not meant that as a compliment. "I beg your pardon?" Icy, disapproving. Every bit the old-maid spinster. Something about it made him wince, as if he'd been reprimanded by his nursemaid.

"Sorry," he muttered. "But I think he dislocated my shoulder."

If he was expecting sympathy from the earl's daughter in the ball gown, he was destined for disappointment. She only sniffed. "You did try to stab him."

Bram smiled briefly before grabbing Martin again. "Ready?"

"No! For what?"

Too late. Bram had already shoved his shoulder joint back into place with a great crack. Martin paled, choking on a yell.

"Better?" Bram asked.

Martin looked like he might be ill, but when he moved slightly, he only winced. "Yes, actually."

"Wrap that up in a sling. You'll be fine." Bram stepped back. "Don't be sick on my boots."

"I won't." Martin was shaky but regaining his color. He was tall, rather handsome. And clearly frantic.

"Who told you about the red dove?" Clara asked, handing Bram the whiskey. He accepted it with surprised appreciation, as if it had been a very long time since someone thought of his wellbeing. "It's not rum," she said. "Isn't that what sailors drink?"

"You're thinking pirates again, lass."

He was smiling again, just for her. It made her feel invincible. It was a struggle to turn to Martin, who was turning his neckcloth into a sling, teeth gritted. He was the approximate color of boiled fish. "You know Miss Taunton, don't you?" she asked.

Martin nodded as Bram tossed back his whiskey and took up his usual spot near the door.

"What does she look like?" Clara asked.

"Dark hair, boundless energy. A bit terrifying, actually."

"And a beauty mark under her left eye?"

"Her right eye."

Clara nodded, satisfied he had passed the test. "Very well. Why are you running around trying to stab people, Martin? Did she put you up to it?" It was absolutely something Sybil would do.

"Not exactly." Martin sank onto a bench. Clara handed him a cup of tea with extra honey. If he passed out now, they'd never get any information. "She was supposed to meet me here with Heloise. But they never showed. It's been a week now."

"Why were they meeting you here?"

"So Heloise and I could run away to Gretna Green and get married. He kept her confined to that house. Wouldn't let any visitors see her. There was a lock on the attic, where she slept. Did you know that?"

"How did you manage to see her often enough to want to marry her, then?" Bram asked.

"My father was the marquis's solicitor," Martin explained. "I inherited the job, despite not wanting it. The marquis has many estates, thousands and thousands of acres, most of it unentailed. It requires a lot of paperwork. So does having a ward. Several wards."

"Miss Blanche Yarwood?" Clara asked.

"Yes, though she's away at present. I've never met her."

"What of Lady Rosalinde?"

"I've never heard the name."

"Would your father know?"

"Yes, probably, if she stayed with the marquis or had anything to do with him, legally speaking."

"She was his ward as well."

"Then definitely yes, but he's a gone a bit funny with age. He doesn't remember *me* sometimes. Sybil said she had papers for me. Evidence that the marquis was up to no good."

"But she never showed."

"No. Neither has Heloise. And no one at the Hall knows anything. At least, no one who would talk to *me*."

"Are his footmen new?" Clara asked.

Martin frowned. "I don't know. There are more then I remember. Maybe? Why?"

"Whatever job they are performing, it is not the work of a footman."

"It's the work of hired muscle," Bram elaborated.

Martin paled. "Heloise."

"You love her?"

"With my very soul."

Bram raised an eyebrow. "And her dowry?"

Martin straightened, which took some doing. Pain tightened his mouth. "Only someone who has never met her could suggest such a thing."

"Or someone who's seen a bit more of the world than you, lad."

"All the same, I love her. *Her.* She's witty and caring and smarter than you and I put together. She is an astronomer. I've already drawn up the contract that guarantees she keeps her lands. I drew it up before I realized what the marquis was truly like. How little he cared. I hoped it would convince him."

"We will find Heloise," Clara declared, as forcefully as she knew how. As if it would make it true. "And then we will ask her what *she* wants."

When Bess returned for the tray, she also had news that all the rooms at the inn were let but the storm was not abating. She offered them the parlor and the fire, and Clara would have gratefully accepted had Bram not stared at Martin, who finally came back to himself with a self-deprecating smile. "Forgive me, Lady Clara—you may, of course, have my room tonight."

Bram inclined his head, very much like a captain who would expect no less from one of his sailors. He led the way up the narrow staircase and insisted on checking the room, including under the bed. When he was satisfied that it was safe, he asked if Bess could see to a bath for Clara.

Much as Bram seemed never to have someone set aside a warming drink because they knew he would be cold, Clara had never had someone order a bath to see to her comforts. She sat on the edge of the coverlet as a young man hauled buckets of hot water up the stairs for her. There were clean towels, candles burning in the window seat, and faded murals of oak leaves and stags leaping over the walls.

And only one bed.

She tried not to focus on it.

"I can wait outside the door if you prefer," Bram said. "But I'll sleep in this chair tonight. I'm not leaving you alone."

"You can stay," she said shyly. "You can't be any warmer than I am in your wet things."

"I'm used to it." Bram sat in the chair by the fire, which he had stoked to a cheerful roar. It only smoked a little. The rain was a steady tap on the roof. He leaned back, legs spread, glass of whiskey in his hand, watching her with those inscrutable eyes as she made her way to the privacy screen.

"Will you tell me about it?" she asked. "About being on a ship? The places you've seen?"

Even though he could not see her, as she removed her gown, she was aware of every single inch of her skin. Bess had helped her with her laces before leaving them alone. Her ball gown was draped over the second chair, and she laid her chemise over the top of the screen, followed by her stockings. Bram made a noise from the other side, which she could not interpret.

She stood naked, knowing he was just there, just in reach. Knowing what it felt like to have those strong fingers stroke between her legs, the hot pull of his mouth on her neck. It was intoxicating, desperately tempting.

She shivered as she finally stepped into the steaming bathwater. Bess had left a dish of soap, a washcloth, and rose oil for her hair, which must have been very dear to her. Rose oil was something the Nightingale might wear, not Miss Vinegar. Clara decided to use just a drop, not enough to waste, just enough to hint at something that was not proper and prim and nutritional, like water biscuits. A *hint* of the Nightingale.

"What did you want to know?" he asked, his voice deepening.

"How long were you at sea?" She let a drop of rose oil fall into the water, scenting the steam, her pinkening skin, the small, simple room.

"Years. Since I was a lad working my way up, and then for most of the war."

The war alone had taken twelve years. "Did you miss London?"

He snorted. "No."

She had to smile. "Not even a little bit?"

"I missed my sisters and my wee niece, who don't live in London anymore, thank Christ. And a particular coffee from a small Turkish spot at the very back of Covent Garden. They make it with cinnamon, I think. And other spices."

"It sounds delicious." She'd never had cinnamon in the coffee. She made a note to try it as soon as was possible. She did not think the inn would have cinnamon on hand.

She ran the washcloth over herself and contemplated washing her hair, but decided against having to deal with the wet mess of it all the night long.

"Were you at Trafalgar? With Admiral Nelson."

"Aye."

"That must have been very exciting."

"That's one word for it."

"Is that where you got your scars?"

"Which ones?" he asked drily.

"I'm sorry, I don't mean to pry."

"They are not well received in fancy drawing rooms."

It was her turn for a dry tone. "I can assure you that your scars are not off-putting to the ladies." She'd seen proof of it with the way they watched him, the way they sometimes sighed behind their fans.

All of which she was also guilty of.

"What about the scar on your cheek?"

"Splinters from a cannonball that landed too close. Mostly we harried the privateers hired by the French to bedevil us. Sometimes down to Bermuda and the islands. Sometimes we waited offshore to lend a hand when the army was pushed too far back. Often we were part of the convoys delivering everything from grain to horses. Who do not much like the open sea, by the way."

"I can imagine not. But I can see you perfectly suited to protect Wellington and his men. I would want you at my back."

She sank further into the bath and could not help a sigh of pleasure as the warmth released the tension in the muscles and the last of the chill that had seeped into her bones.

Bram shifted in his chair. There was the creak of floorboards as he walked toward her, closer, closer. He paused on the other side of the screen. "Clara?" he asked roughly.

"Yes?"

"Tell me to go."

She did not want him to go. She wanted him to stay. More

than stay—she wanted him to breach the carved wooden panel that separated them. Even though she was still reclining nude in the bath.

Especially because she was still reclining nude in the bath.

"Don't go."

A harsh intake of breath, and then she wondered if he really would go.

He did not.

He came around the screen, huge and powerful, outlined by the gold light of the candles. She stared back at him mutely, her own breath catching in her throat. He knelt at the side of the tub, shirt sleeves rolled up. His arms were as muscled as she'd imagined, dusted with dark hair. The surface of the bathwater rippled when he trailed his fingers through it, skimming her knee, the top of her thigh.

"I'm not an earl's son—not a single baron in the family tree, even," he said.

"I know that."

"I was born north of Inverness. Not a starched cravat to be seen."

She tilted her head. "I know that too, Bram."

His hand stilled on her leg, then slipped between her thighs. "Say it again."

"What?"

"My name."

"Bram."

She was rewarded with a stroke closer to the molten center of her, aching for his touch, which he refused to give fully. His thumb dragged close to the crease at the top of the thigh and hipbone. She gasped, just a little.

"And I'm too old for you."

She frowned. "Don't be ridiculous. You're not that old." She had no idea how told he was, and she did not give a fig.

"I'm forty-two."

"So?"

"So, too old for you."

"I'm twenty-nine years old. In debutante years, that's nearly a hundred. I'm older than *you*."

His mouth quirked. "Is that so? I never did understand London mathematics."

"No one does." She decided to be brave and reached out to touch his arm. The muscles and tendons shifted under her hand. His skin was cold. "You're still chilled!"

"A wet December night in the Highlands is chilly," he said. "A ride through Hampshire barely rates."

"You could warm up in here with me."

It had taken a considerable bout of courage to say that out loud. Desire threatened to topsy-turvy her good sense. Good riddance to it.

He raised an eyebrow. "I'm not fitting in there with you, lass."

It was not a particularly large tub, but she felt certain they could manage.

"I can't take you to balls, you know, or Almack's," he said abruptly. "Scottish sailors aren't on the guest list, captains or not."

"Do you promise?"

He smiled wider. She did not. A horrible thought seized her. He was trying to talk her out of whatever this might be. Talk *himself* out of it. The night in the caves was a result of unusual circumstances, to say the least. The moment in the attic was in order to distract whoever was coming up the stairs to discover them.

It wasn't about *her*. Of course it wasn't.

She was an absolute idiot.

"There it is again," he said softly. "The posture."

"You should go if you don't want this," she said evenly. "I won't try to convince you." She *wanted* to, but she wouldn't. Just once she wanted someone to pick her. She wanted *Bram* to pick her. "It's quite all right, really," she said. "We're adults, and we've been in many oddly intimate circumstances."

She made to scoot back, trying to preserve any shred of dignity. She was suddenly too exposed, and it had nothing to do with her lack of clothes.

His hand tightened on her thigh. "Clara, look at me."

She did not want to. She did not want to hear his reasons, however sound they might be. She was not enough. And *that* was enough.

"Clara." A quiet command, but a command all the same. She glanced at him. "You think I don't want you?"

She tilted her chin, refused to answer. He searched her face and then stood abruptly. She would not cry. It was ridiculous to cry. This was exactly what she'd expected.

Until Bram pulled his shirt off and began to undo the buttons of his breeches.

CHAPTER TWENTY-ONE

CAPTAIN BRAM THORN was looming over her, stripping off his clothing.

All of his clothing.

He was even more striking than she had imagined, and she had a *very* good imagination. She was famous for it, actually. Infamous, even.

He was so powerful. He exuded the kind of gentle strength that never made her feel nervous, only protected. Thick thighs, a wide chest, all covered in hair and lined with scars. Tattooed as well, with a swallow on each pectoral.

And all focused entirely on her. Small, pale, forgettable Clara Prescott.

"Move over," he said. "You'll wish you never suggested it when it rains down into the rooms below us and they toss us into the streets in our towels." He stepped into the tub and maneuvered himself behind her, stretching out his legs on either side of her. "Mind your toes."

She giggled. She actually giggled. Then she clapped her hands over her mouth. The Nightingale wouldn't giggle. There was nothing sultry about *giggling*. But somehow, he always managed to make her to do it.

Bram only touched her wrists, lowering her arms. "I want to hear all of the sounds you make," he said against her ear. He pulled her back against his chest, sloshing the warm water around them, dripping over the edge, as predicted. The hardness of his cock rose against her spine. "Do you still think I don't want you?" he murmured.

She shook her head.

"Good girl."

She licked her lips, melting against him. He laid one arm on the lip of the tub, and the other disappeared into the water. He brushed against her quim, softly teasing her, even as he bit down on her earlobe. The contrast made her jolt, shooting sensation from her nipples to her bud. "Do you think I don't dream about the caves, about you coming on my fingers? Hot and clenching and moaning?"

Just as she was moaning now, because he was parting her lips, stroking up and down, a light circle around her bud, the scrape of his teeth against her throat. She clutched at his thighs, trying to twist around to touch him, finally.

"You come for me first," he said. "Just like this."

"Bram."

"Just for me, pirate. And then I'll take every part of you into my mouth."

She arched back, maddened with the pressure building so swiftly. "What if I want you in *my* mouth?"

He chuckled softly. "Oh, now you've done it, pirate."

He delved into her softness, plunging his fingers deep until she gasped helplessly. He used his other hand to stroke and circle her bud, straining and swelling for him. Circle and stroke, circle and stroke—until the pleasure of it peaked, sudden and sharp. She jerked, and the water rippled around her breasts.

"I want to touch you now," she said.

"Oh, sweetheart, we've just begun."

He climbed out of the tub and helped her to her feet, drying her off in slow brushes with the towel. She felt exposed again, taken care of. She didn't know what to do with the feelings—they were so new to her. She ran her fingertips over his shoulders as he continued to dry her, down his biceps, across his chest. She was fascinated by those tattoos, scraped her nails over them. "What do these mean?"

"A swallow tattoo for every five thousand miles sailed," he answered, far more interested in stroking every part of her. "Hold fast so we don't fall overboard, so we always have something to hold on to."

"Are all sailors superstitious?"

"Aye. The sea doesn't give up her secrets easily. Like someone else I know."

She leaned down to lick a drop of water on his lower lip. He groaned and captured her mouth in a searing kiss, hard and demanding. "You're going to be the death of me." When she smiled, just a little, he groaned again. "You like that, little pirate."

"Maybe."

"Definitely." He scooped her up into his arms and she yelped, clutching at him for balance. "I've got you," he said. "I've always got you."

He carried her to the bed as the fire still burned merrily, warming the room. The coverlet was thin, but clean. There were tulips in a glass mug on the table. "Not much of a suite," he said. "For the daughter of an earl."

She beamed at him, couldn't help it. He'd be horrified if he ever found out her father had used real gold on the walls of their drawing room. He'd been bored with it after two weeks because it drew too much attention way from him and had it all torn down. "It's perfect."

The shadow that had threatened to cross Bram's face fled. He lowered her to the edge of the back and then crowded her back until she lay for him like an offering. He rubbed his nose along her neck. "You smell like roses and rain. Like wicked things."

She liked that. She liked that very much.

He dragged his lips down to her breast, sucking it deep into his hot, wet mouth. She gasped, writhing beneath him as sensation after sensation shot from her nipples to her quim. He sucked long and hard until she was whimpering, and then he moved to her other breast, giving it the same care. The same dedication.

He was going to drive her mad. On purpose. He was moving so slowly, so methodically.

She'd never thought much about her breasts before, certainly had not considered how sensitive they might be, how she might come to a climax by them alone. She fisted her hands in the sheets, scrabbling for purchase, then raked down his chest, her nails scoring his muscles. He grew harder, pressing along her leg. She reached down, desperate.

"Not yet," he murmured against her wet, puckered nipples. His grip on her wrist was unbreakable. She tugged, nearly frantic. He laughed again, but his jaw was tight, the tendons of his neck standing out. "I'm not done."

"Bram Thorn," she said.

"I'm not done," he repeated.

And then he kissed and nibbled his way from her breasts, down her belly, to the very core of her. He licked at her, sucked her into his mouth, her entire bud like it was a candy, rolling his tongue over it. She was going to come again. Surely not.

Definitely.

Right now. His head delved between her thighs, fingers gripping her hips hard, dimpling her flesh, keeping her pinned for his pleasure. For her pleasure. For pleasure. *So much pleasure.* It coursed through her, sweeping her up, claiming her.

She might have screamed. Just a little.

She definitely screamed.

She tried to care, tried to wonder if she should be embarrassed, and decided it wasn't worth the effort, not when she had a hulking brute of a smug Scotsman between her legs, grinning. Let them talk about her down in the pub, if they heard her over the fiddle and the general din.

Bram lay next to her, wiping his mouth, leaving the grin. She kissed him fiercely, tasting her own desire, wanting to taste his.

Wanting to taste *him*. She did not fool herself into hoping for more than this. And if she only got one night, she intended to make the best of it.

The very best.

She kissed the stubble over his cheek, the scar just there, the other one on his eyebrow. She licked the one of the top of his shoulder. His breath stuttered, cock straining against his abdomen.

She vowed to lick every single scar he had, from his shoulder to his chest, the one on his forearm, the many on his fingers. She bit the ones on his knuckles as well. Found one above his hip that looked as though it had been left by a bullet. She paused.

"It's not sightly," he said in his rough burr. When she glared up at him, he blinked. "What, lass?"

"I want to murder the man who did this to you."

His bewilderment increased, then softened. There was fondness there as well, under the surprise. "Bloodthirsty little thing, aren't you? And you have everyone fooled." He dug his fingers into her hair. "Not me, though."

"Not you." She kissed the scar softly.

"Anyway, he's long gone, I reckon. Trafalgar took a fair few of us on either side. Has us still, even those who survived. Now open your legs for me, pirate," he ordered. "Wider. That's it." He settled between them. "Good girl."

She was still wet for him, and he slid to the hilt, keeping that slow, maddening pace. Sliding deep, pulling back, and then sliding even deeper. She angled her hips up, urging him to go faster, harder. And then his ironclad control finally loosened and he plunged into her, driving her up the mattress, claiming her completely. The sound of their bodies meeting, the sweat gathering at the small of her back, the fierce burn of his eyes, the ruthless rhythm, the gentle hands—it was all Bram, all hers. Just for now.

When his own climax took him, hers followed, chasing each other's, pulling them up another peak, and another. Dropping them back to the earth sweaty and panting and sated.

CHAPTER TWENTY-TWO

CLARA DID NOT want to go back to the lavish, extravagant Eastbourne Hall. She did not want silver tea trays and French champagne and thick, luxurious rugs underfoot. She did not want perfume and lady's maids and waltzes. She wanted to stay right here in this inn that smelled like smoke and roasting meat, with the thin sheets and the cold draft sneaking in under the door.

With Bram.

Her experience was minimal, despite her exhaustive research and writing of naughty books. Even so, she could not have imagined such a night. Her body no longer felt like it belonged to her. It turned toward Bram even now in the bed, even as her brain reminded her that this would not last.

The heat thrumming through her just at a glance of his bare, muscled chest dusted with hair, the line of his jaw, all had a counterargument: if it would not last, she should enjoy as much as she could for as long as she could.

Decorated naval captains did not marry prim spinsters.

But maybe they had affairs with them.

"You're thinking entirely too hard," Bram murmured, without opening his eyes.

"How can you tell?"

"I just can. You would have made a decent ship's coxswain,

never deviating from your course."

She frowned slightly. "Is that what you think?" Staid, predictable.

"Yes." He cracked one eye open. "And it gives me great pleasure to sidetrack you." He tugged her closer abruptly, sliding her across the sheets until she was pressed against his naked body. She gave a startled giggle. "That's my favorite sound." He nuzzled under her jaw, his beard tickling her sensitive skin. "Well, *one* of them."

He slipped his muscular leg between hers, widening her thighs, brushing against the core of her, all while dragging open-mouthed kisses along her throat. She sighed. "That's another one."

His fingers delved between her legs, teasing. The sigh turned to a thready gasp.

"Better and better."

She was already half mad with desire for him, squirming against him, moaning, when his clever tattooed fingers began their exploration in earnest. They were callused from years of sailing, of pulling ropes and whatever else he had done before working his way up to captain. "You feel so good," he said in his morning-rough voice. She wanted to drink it like whiskey. It burned and went to her head. "So warm and soft."

She was rapidly losing her ability to focus again. He did that to her. So easily.

Not this time. This time he would moan her name.

She squirmed away, sliding down his body.

"Where are you going, little pirate?"

She kissed each inked swallow, following the thick pelt of his hair down his stomach to his cock, already hardening. The sheets fell over her, a private tent to shield her blushes. She licked his hipbone, then bit it. He jerked, saying her name in a filthy voice that shot heat straight to her quim.

She loved it.

She loved the taste of him, salty and clean, the tickle of his hair over her nose, her forehead. The feel of his soft skin over the hardness of his cock, jerking in response as she gave little, teasing licks to the tip bobbing toward her. When she finally drew him between her lips, he tasted salty and clean. He was smooth, hot under her tongue. He swore as she explored him, the silky steel of this length, the rounded tip, back again. He thrust slightly into her mouth. She moaned in response.

The jut of his hips, stuttering as he worked to control himself. His hands in her hair, just this side of too rough—she loved that most of all. She took him as far back into her throat as she could whenever he groaned her name like a prayer. Filthy again, but devout too.

And then he was hauling her up out of the nest of warm sheets, pushing her onto her back, breath harsh, eyes wild.

And she decided she loved that best of al.

"The death of me," he said, pulling her off and hauling her up so he could cover her with his big, hard body. He kissed her deep and slow, rubbing his cock against her quim until she was writhing again, wet and swollen and demanding. "Now," she said, letting her thighs fall open as wide as they could. *"Now, Bram."*

"I lied," he said against her, even as he slid into her warmth, stealing her breath for a moment. She clenched around him deliciously. "That one's my favorite."

He pushed deeper, and she rose to meet every thrust, chasing his retreats, inviting his return. The pace matched her heartbeat until she couldn't feel anything but him. Her thoughts fled and there was only their bodies joining, the rattle of the bed, the panting and gasping. And then the release. It claimed her in waves that arched her back and stole her breath. Her legs stayed wrapped around him, heels digging into his buttocks. His sweaty chest pressed against her. "I'll crush you, lass."

"Yes, please."

"You're made of glass and moonlight."

"I won't break." She nuzzled him, could not help herself. "You always smell like lime candies."

"Occupational hazard."

"How's that?"

"I spent years at sea eating limes to fend off scurvy," he explained. "I developed a taste for it. But limes are not readily available in London."

"Hence lime candies."

"Hence lime candies," he confirmed. "You, on the hand, smell like bergamot, like the best cup of tea on a rainy day." His mouth moved down her throat, over her clavicles. "I could drink you down." A suck, a nibble at her breast, slow and deliberate. Almost lazy. "I don't think they'll miss us for a while yet, do you?"

WHEN THEY RETURNED to Eastbourne Hall it was to find Kitty setting up a table under the grand staircase. Her auburn curls fell out of their pins as she sorted through the contents of a large trunk with leather straps, laying out books over a tablecloth painted with gold griffins.

"Kitty?" Clara stopped in her tracks.

Kitty stopped, turned around. Her eyes widened. "Oh, thank *God*," she said fervently. "A friendly face."

"What are you doing here?"

Kitty smirked. "As the only official purveyor of the Nightingale's books, the marquis invited me to set up a book corner for her new release. Exclusive before the rest of London. Otherwise it's mostly Byron's poetry and the more lascivious books, it has to be said." She dropped her voice. "I've been told there are also dancers and acrobats on their way."

"I am not surprised. But where are you sleeping?"

"There is a small parlor with a settee. It will do for one night."

Clara hugged her, dropping her voice. "Lock your door."

She and Bram crossed the lawn to the dower house next. The sun had come out briefly, and the world outside gleamed prettily.

Selene sat at the table, its lace cloth fluttering in the breeze of the open windows. "I hope you don't mind," she said. "I helped myself to your tray. I don't think Mrs. Meadows likes me as much as she likes your captain. I had only toast and jam before you came."

"I'm not sure she likes anyone as much as she likes the captain," Clara replied with a smile. The captain in question was sitting outside again, after having thoroughly checked the house for knife-wielding foes. Martin had remained in Fitcher, trying to avoid the local authorities and the marquis's men. It was rather frowned upon to try to murder a marquis.

When the rain started a soft patter on the windows, Selene glanced at the door. "Will he not come in?"

"He likes the rain. I suppose it makes sense, after all those years spent outside in various degrees of damp."

Selene shook her head. "Ghastly." She ate another decadent macaron. It was flavored with almonds and rosewater and sat next to hard rolls, a bowl of yesterday's syllabub, and plain scones. It was an odd assortment.

"Did Mrs. Meadows bring this herself?" Clara asked, feeling something niggling in the back of her head.

"One of the footmen," Selene said with a wrinkle of her nose. "One of the ones that seem a bit menacing for a country footman."

"You noticed that too?"

"It's my job to notice things."

"I suppose it is."

"Not to show off," Selene added, "though I do love to, but I can tell, for instance, that you had quite the evening."

"I did see a man nearly stabbed."

"Pish." She waved that away. "I thought we were becoming friends, however unlikely for an earl's daughter and someone like me."

"We are," Clara said. She liked the other woman. She was straightforward and funny.

"Then why are you fobbing that pathetic lie off on me?" Selene grinned. "I know I well-pleasured woman when I see one."

Clara pressed her palms to her warm cheeks. "Is it that obvious?"

Selene shrugged elegantly. "My job, remember?"

"I know I'm not supposed to."

"Supposed to what? Be happy?" Selene outright snorted at that. "There are a thousand things we're not supposed to do. From what I can tell, you especially should do all of them."

"What does that mean?"

"It means you deserve a little fun. You have the patience of a saint for not stabbing half the people here with your fish fork."

"He's not like anyone I've ever known," Clara admitted quietly, reaching for a scone.

"You are still blushing. Good for you. Good for him."

"I know it can't last, but…"

"We don't know anything, not really. After all, should I be sitting here over tea with an earl's daughter? Invited to supper at a marquis's table?" Selene broke off a piece of scone as well. "These are truly terrible, though, I must admit. Even considering what Mrs. Meadows thinks of me."

Clara was thinking the same thing. Yesterday's scones were drizzled with caramel sauce and served with chocolate pudding dressed with strawberries. These were plain and dry and there was no butter. The tray held enough food for several people, but not the kind generally delivered to guests. Thin beef tea, the end of a chunk of cheese. No delicate bone china here—the plates were glazed brown ceramic.

"Did you see the footman go back to the Hall?" she asked, frowning.

"I think he went that way. I wasn't paying much attention. Why?"

"Just wondering." Clara looked out the window where Selene

had motioned. The path led back to the Hall, diverting once into the gardens and again toward the grotto. What if this food wasn't meant for them? What if it was supposed to be delivered to women no one was supposed to know about—say, a ward and her chaperone locked up somewhere on the estate?

"How well do you know the marquis?" Clara asked. She had no proof, only that sense of instinct prodding her.

Selene popped a strawberry into her mouth. She made everything look effortless elegant and sensual, even with her shoes kicked off and her feet drawn under her. "Not terribly well."

"When did he hire you?"

"He didn't."

Clara turned away from her perusal of the paths leading from the dower house. "He didn't?"

"Devil hired me and my house. He usually does. The marquis just likes to act as though everything is his idea. Why did *you* come here, if you don't mind my asking?"

If she wanted Selene to share confidences, Clara supposed she should as well. "I had a friend who was visiting, and I haven't heard from her in a while." She shrugged, not nearly as elegantly as Selene had. "And truthfully, ordinarily I would never be invited to a party like this. I wanted to see what the fuss was about."

"And?"

"And mostly I'd rather be in the library with a good book."

Selene laughed. "Me too." She waggled her eyebrows. "Except for the grotto, of course."

"Um…"

She laughed harder. "There's no need to be ashamed."

"I'm not. Exactly. It's just…my reputation."

"Ah yes, the holy reputation of a lady. I remember it well enough. It was dismal and exceedingly tiresome."

"You do?"

"I am a viscount's youngest daughter," Selene said. "Or was, before he disowned me. After I ran away with a very handsome lad who was very good at lying and had no intention of taking us all the way to Gretna Green."

"I hope you made him suffer."

"Eventually." She poured more tea into her cup. "His wife is very pretty. And she likes me best."

"Would you ever…" Clara hoped she wasn't about to cause offense. None of her books dealt with the etiquette of a conversation like this. "Would you ever consider telling me what you know of the marquis? What his rooms look like?" She must sound mad. "Anything unusual, say?"

Selene paused, then looked delighted. "You're a Spinster!"

"That's hardly news."

"No, a *Spinster*."

Clara blinked. "You've heard of us?"

"Of course I have. I'm quite jealous, you know. I did a bit of espionage during the war, but it sounds much more interesting to take down those who want to keep us in cages."

"You must know all about them. The men on our lists. Some of the ladies too."

Selene nodded. "More than I'd like, mostly. But a woman has to eat. I do not care for hunger. Or sewing."

"Would you help me? If it weren't dangerous? I would pay, of course."

Selene tilted her head, watching her for a long moment. "Yes, I think I would. And do you know why?"

Clara shook her head.

"Because you haven't once looked down your nose at me, Lady Clara Prescott. I can't tell you how rare that is."

"I feel the same way, I assure you. You haven't looked down your nose at *me*."

Selene winked. "And it sounds like fun."

"I might have…other questions." Questions the Nightingale wanted answered.

"Everyone does."

Clara could not ask them, though they crowded on her tongue. Mrs. Meadows laughed from the doorstep.

"She's sweet on him." Selene smiled.

Mrs. Meadows knocked before entering, followed by a maid-servant bearing a new tray. This one was heaped with dishes of coddled eggs and ham and potatoes roasted with chives, all on painted porcelain.

She clicked her tongue at the tray already on the table. "Now who in the world brought you this?"

"One of the footmen," Clara replied.

"That lot," Mrs. Meadows grumbled. "I don't mind saying, I don't know how they train them in London, but this is not how we do things here. This looks better suited to the servant hall. My apologies."

"Are there many new footmen?" Clara asked.

"We've had to hire dozens of new folk from the village and the town," Mrs. Meadows replied. "For such a big party."

"Of course." Something about that would not stop knocking inside Clara's head. "Thank you, Mrs. Meadows."

Clara immediately put down her tea in favor of prowling through the garden like a child searching for hidden presents. She knew she must look ridiculous, crawling between the hedges, crouching in the bushes. She found footprints in the mud, still damp from the storm, but they did not lead anywhere interesting, not even to the grotto. Frustration simmered in her belly. She knew she was close to something. She could *feel* it. She just did not know what it was.

Girls go missing at Eastbourne Hall.

Chapter Twenty-Three

I N THE EVENING, the ladies gathered in the yellow drawing room for whist and wine after supper.

It was exactly as dismal as Clara expected. Mostly because she despised whist. The ladies did not trouble her much. She did not know if that was because she was simply too busy to bother with their disdain or if her slowly burgeoning confidence lent her an extra shield. She had created her persona and perhaps leaned too far into the acerbic, disapproving aspects. She could hardly expect people to befriend her when she would not befriend herself. No one wanted to be judged.

But whatever it was that sent a bit more starch into her spine certainly was not her dress, exactly as plain and serviceable as all of her others.

Useful, though, as it turned out. Very, very useful.

She took a turn about the room and, glancing into the hall, could see directly into the servant stair. Someone had left the door open as well, with a basket of fresh laundry on the step.

It was nothing for Clara, in that perfectly plain dress, to dart out, scoop it up on her hip, and climb up to the family wing.

A footman—a proper footman—that was, even rushed past her and took no notice. A nod of the head and on to work. He didn't stop long enough to question whether or not she was actually a maid. There it was again, that thrill of success, the lure of accomplishing some secret quest under the noses of those who judged most harshly: fortune hunters, powerful men looking for biddable wives, dowagers trying to secure any measure of control over their lives as the expense of others.

She understood now why Peony raced horses, why Sybil leapt into every experience, why Matilda stole ball invitations. Sneaking up the servant stair might not be akin to climbing down the outside of a mansion in Mayfair, but in this case it was just as dangerous. Certainly more practical.

And it wasn't raining on her head, which was most helpful.

The family wing was laid with plush carpet runners, painted oil lamps, busts of Roman ladies on pedestals. Rococo plaster-work and rose details marched across the ceiling, all of it converging in the master bedroom. It was easy to pick out the marquis's chamber. The door was painted the same famous blue of his coats.

Clara's basket contained fresh bed linens and what might be bathing towels. Nothing that would be out of place being delivered to his chamber. She knocked once, and when no reply was forthcoming, she cast one last look down each hallway and ducked inside.

The marquis's chamber was far less ostentatious than she would have assumed. It was luxurious, of course, but nothing like the mess of textures and colors preferred by her father. There were no gold swans holding up the bed curtains, for one thing. Her father had loved them dearly. More than he loved her mother, to be sure.

Mahogany chairs circled the marble fireplace and a chaise longue waited under one of the windows. Thick blue brocade curtains fell to the floor. There were gold candlesticks every-where, a table for decanters of brandy and port, a bathing room set back behind a door painted with a frieze of the Roman countryside.

Clara went straight to the bathing room to make certain no one was being kept inside. It was empty. She knocked on the walls for good measure, listening for hollow spots. She peered under the cushions and the mattress and discovered more than she ever wanted to know about the marquis's bedsports, along with two debt vowels crumpled in the back of the fireplace. There were books, some naughtier than others.

And then, finally, under the false bottom of the drawer of his washstand: a key.

Clara was amassing quite the collection.

She added it to the ribbon of keys around her neck and tucked them all into the safety of her stays.

Just as the door opened.

Panic seized her.

Selene waltzed in, dragging the marquis behind her. "My lord, you are terrible."

She froze, spotting Clara. They stared at each other for a moment that felt like a hundred years. Clara dove behind the nearest curtain, heart hammering in her throat.

Selene turned to the marquis, leading him toward the bed, keeping him facing away from the rest of the room. He was a little inebriated, but not nearly enough to forget anything he might see. For instance, the basket of laundry he nearly tripped over. "Who the devil left this here?"

Selene turned him in tiny increments with a hand on his arm, a flip of her hair, all to draw him away from Clara inexpertly hidden in direct eyeline behind the blasted basket. The irony—she was usually so good at disappearing.

"I'll have them sacked," the marquis seethed, covering his embarrassment over a trip of the foot. Behind his back, Selene rolled her eyes at Clara.

"My lord," she said, pouting, "you brought me here so you would not have to share me, and now you concern yourself with trivialities."

Clara eased from behind the thick brocade.

"My feelings will be quite hurt."

The marquis reached for her. Clara did not trust his smile.

"Can't have that, my dear."

Clara made it to the door, the key burning in her stays, her pulse so loud in her ears she wondered they did not hear it.

In the safety of the hall, she finally took a proper breath.

And found she could not leave Selene trapped in that room with that man.

She knew the other woman could take care of herself, no doubt had tricks such as the Spinsters used with herbs and laudanum. Still. There had to be something she could do, however temporarily. A little mouse causing havoc in the larder.

She could not think of a message that would draw him out of Selene's arms, even if she could find someone to deliver it in time. She would have to use what she had on hand.

An oil lamp, a tapestry.

Fire was always a risk. It could devour a house long before it was discovered.

It could not happen to a better man.

She put out the wick and poured the oil from the lamp on a tapestry she pulled from the wall. Then she fed it under the door and crumpled it into a corner, leaving space enough to Selene to escape, if she could not choose the shelter of the balcony. One of the candles from the fluted sconces polished daily to a shine. A tip of the hand.

The flame caught right away, racing through the fabric, dark smoke pouring off it. Clara raced to the top of the servant stairs and yelled. "Fire! Fire in the master's chambers!"

At the sound of the pounding footsteps rushing up and the shouts for water, Clara went in the opposite direction. She popped out into the garden and crossed the lawn at a dead run, grinning like a fool.

Right into the arms of Bram.

"What did I tell you would happen if you went out there alone?"

CHAPTER TWENTY-FOUR

His voice was deep and faintly ominous. She felt it everywhere. She swayed toward him like a sunflower tuned to the stars instead of the sun. Like one of his ship's compasses, always pointing north.

"I was in the ladies' drawing room."

He bent closer, eyes narrowed. "Little liar—that's not the only place you've been."

She blinked at him. "What?"

"You smell like fire," he said. "And someone just threw a burning tapestry off the marquis's balcony, mere moments after you raced across the lawn like you were being chased by dogs."

She licked her lips. "Oh. That."

"Yes. *That.*"

"It was very much worth it," she said, pulling out her ribbon of keys. "The marquis had this one hidden in his bedroom."

"His bedroom," he said. "Where you lit a fire?"

"I only wanted to give Selene a chance for him to find someone else for the night."

"He was *there?*" Bram's vaunted calmness turned sharp.

She tried to smile. "He didn't see me."

He closed his eyes.

"And I have this!" Clara waved the key at him again.

He opened his eyes again just in time to see the latest blackmail note, which she had tucked into her cuff to inspect later. It touched his boot, and he bent to pick it up before she could stop him.

It had, of course, landed face-up.

Five thousand pounds or I share your secret. Devil's Night by the lion fountain. Leave it and walk away.

Bram straightened slowly. His face turned to cold, impassive stone, but his eyes burned. If she had thought he was angry before, it was nothing to this. Dark waters seethed and boiled below his surface. "What is this?"

She tried to smile again, as if it was all perfectly normal. "It's nothing."

She reached for the note, but he would not let her have it. It crinkled as his grip tightened. He visibly forced himself to loosen it. "Someone is threatening you?"

"I'm sure it will come to nothing." She realized immediately that making light of the situation was the wrong tactic. Entirely. She knew what he looked like now, when the battle was upon him. Fierce, terrifying. Though it was not aimed at her, she shivered nonetheless. This was a man who would do whatever it took. Rules and decorum meant nothing to him. He was a protector through and through, and he had been woken without warning.

"You didn't tell me," he said evenly. Too evenly. "You're being blackmailed and *you didn't tell me?*"

She swallowed, lifted her chin. "I am handling it."

"How?"

She wrinkled her nose. Here was where her argument fell spectacularly apart. Because she had not been handling it at all. She was ignoring it and hoping it would go away. "I've been busy."

"You've been *busy?*" He prowled even closer. There was no other word for it.

"Yes," she said stubbornly. "You may recall we are trying to find two missing ladies. Four, if Sybil's letter is correct."

"And why are they more important than you?" he asked quietly, all deadly menace. A storm cloud waiting to break.

"They just are." She shrugged helplessly.

"*They are not.*" He closed his hands around her elbows, dragging her closer so that she had to tilt her head back to meet his gaze. It was fire and stone and iron.

"They are more urgent, then." She blinked at his icy fury. "*I'm* fine. *They* might not be."

"Clara, this man threatened you. He knows where you are. And then you went traipsing through the house without me, against my express orders."

"But I'm fine." She was a little warm, actually. She'd never had anyone defend her so staunchly, even from herself. "Truly."

"Not good enough. Who is he?"

"Don't you think that if I knew that, I would have done something about it already?"

His eyes closed briefly. "Alone." It wasn't a question.

"I suppose."

He blanched. "Tell me this is the first message you've gotten."

She winced. "One at my house, one delivered to me on the street a messenger boy. Another here at the Hall."

He did not reply for a moment. His jaw clenched so hard she was half afraid he would crack it right off. "I really will turn you over my knee."

"Promises, promises." She'd already forgotten that trying to make a joke of her situation was only going to make it worse.

"Is that so?" He crowded into the tiny sliver of space left between them. Too late she realized she had nowhere to go. There was hunger under his banked fury. Desire.

For her.

"Is that what you want?" he demanded.

She swallowed, lust and anticipation chasing through her blood.

"Answer me, Clara." A dark growl. It tightened her nipples,

jolting sensation between her thighs. She would not have thought that she did want this, but her body clearly craved it. His quiet, dominating touch. Her mind marveled at the fact that she trusted this man enough to explore her own desires.

But she did not know how to say it out loud. Were she someone else, she might have flirted, might have said something provoking just for the fun of knowing she had instigated that in him. Her characters would have done any of these things. Would have undressed right then and there.

And why couldn't she? If she wanted her private life to be different from her public life, she was going to have to act. If she wanted Bram, she was going to have to act.

And she did want Bram.

Again. Still. Always.

And as the clock was ticking on their relationship, she could not afford to waste any time. She could not afford decorum and etiquette and rules.

So she reached behind to pull her laces loose, until her dress pooled at her feet. It was the sound of the fabric hitting the floor that had Bram hissing out a breath, proving he was not unaffected. She took off her chemise cover, until she stood in her stays and stockings and little red ribbons.

Anticipation was electric between them.

"Are you breaking the rules, Clara?" he asked silkily. He towered over her.

She lifted her chin, but her hands trembled with the need to touch him. To feel him touch her.

He laughed once, softly. The way she imagined a pirate might laugh.

And then he spun her around, bending her over the tea table. She gasped, the inlaid wood cool and smooth on her bare skin. He was at her back, fully dressed, his big hand pressing between her shoulder blades. She was already wet, already full of fire.

"Are you sorry for putting yourself in danger?"

She shook her head silently, defiantly.

"Wrong answer, lass."

He caressed her backside gently, one cheek, then the other. She felt like a harp string, reverberating after being plucked. Waiting for the next note in the song.

His mouth brushed her ear, sending goosebumps across her sensitive skin. "If you want to stop, you say so."

She nodded.

"Out loud, Clara. Say it. Say, 'I understand, Bram.'"

"I understand, Bram," she said on a tiny moan of desperation.

"And do you understand that you don't face the world alone? Not anymore?"

"Yes." She was melting and burning all at once. It was nearly too much.

"I'm not sure I believe you. I think we need to make sure you remember."

She arched back just a little, seeking his touch. Squirming at the throbbing pressure in her quim. Aching. "Yes."

"What was that?"

"Yes, Bram."

He finally touched her, another stroke of his fingers over her bottom, a tease between the lips, and then back again. A hard squeeze. And finally, a light slap. She jumped. Another slap, slightly harder. It didn't hurt, not really. It stung, in a good way that made her writhe and moan. A third slap, his palm connecting with a satisfying crack of sound. She gasped. Her breasts felt fuller, pressed against the table. Her bud swelled, tingled. *"Bram."*

And then there were no words, only mouths and hands and panting breaths as he hauled her up. They came together in a frenzy, pulling at any remaining clothing, kissing all the while. She'd never felt like this, desperate and alive, impatient for more. Wicked. Free.

Clara pulled at the placket of his pants. When he sprang free into her waiting palm, he was hot and hard and it made her moan again, even before his fingers found her, dragging through her slick folds. He strained against her hand, sucking at her throat in short, devastating pulls. It was everything and not nearly enough.

He hiked her up, setting her back against the wall, working her until she was so wet and keening with need. He positioned himself at her entrance, holding still. "Take me inside," he demanded.

She settled on the tip of him, lowering herself carefully. He filled her so thoroughly that she clenched around him until he groaned into her neck. Another inch, and another, until he was fully seated and she was pinned to the wall, filled with his hardness. His big hands spanned her hips, steadying her. "Ride me, pirate," he growled. "Take your pleasure."

She found a pace that made her shiver and whimper, up and down, up and down, stretching to accommodate him, slippery and deep. Little gasps escaped her as she rode him harder and deeper, the coiling low in her belly, searing in its intensity. It built and built until it shattered her and she came with a sob. He groaned into her damp skin, hips stuttering, following her to climax.

They stayed like that for a long moment, panting, before he let her down gently. Her legs were weak, her knees soft. He used his handkerchief to clean her up and then himself before tucking back into his pants. She had mostly regained the feeling in her legs by the time he was finished. He tipped up her chin. "All right?"

She nodded. "Better than all right."

"All the same, you'll indulge me." He swept her up into his arms and carried her to the chair by the low fire. She rested against his chest, listening to the steady, comforting beat of his heart.

"A threat to you is a threat to me, Clara," he said darkly. "And it will not stand."

She tried not to melt, she really did. Was she supposed to be angry? Irritated? Frightened of the blackmailer? How could she be with this man standing with her, fierce and protective? She felt less alone than she ever had before, and it was astonishing.

Incredible. Emotions she could not even name swirled inside her.

She smoothed her hands down his big arms, just because she could. "Thank you."

He frowned. "What now?"

"Thank you for caring. I know it's simply in your nature, but thank you all the same."

He lowered his forehead to hers. "You are infuriating, little pirate. And precious."

"I'm not," she said softly. "And that too is fine."

"You *are*. You're also stubborn and reckless and far too self-deprecating."

"Bram, I know what I am."

He snorted. "You do not." He kissed her, quick and hard. "We do this together."

CHAPTER TWENTY-FIVE

THE DAY LEADING into Devil's Night pulsed with expectation and impatience.

The guests kept mostly to themselves, resting, pampering themselves as more and more carriages rolled up the driveway. Mrs. Meadows sent several trays by harried housemaids. Clara could have constructed a castle of her own out of the shortbread alone.

Bram searched every tray, glowered at every person who dared to walk by. He searched the dower house from top to bottom. He questioned Mrs. Meadows; he talked to the stable master and the footman in charge of delivering messages. He did not find another blackmail note.

Clara laid her two best gowns out on her bed and sighed. Loudly.

Never mind her blackmail and the looming demise of her career. She was going to embarrass herself at Devil's Night. Guests had been instructed to wear red. Clara did not own a red dress. The best she could do was wrap a red bandeau around her hair and ribbons through the tops of her gloves.

It shouldn't matter. There were so many more important things to worry about. Abduction, the rules of card games she had memorized but never actually played, blackmail.

A plan she had not shared with Bram.

But even so, she wanted him to remember her as anything but a pale waif of a woman ignored by others. Just this once. Despite her best efforts, it rankled.

On top of it all, she was still short one red stocking ribbon. She had searched everywhere.

"Well, that won't do," Selene said from the doorway.

Clara wrinkled her nose. "I know."

Selene sized her up. "I have a dress that will fit you with a little alteration. Nothing we can't handle."

"Oh, I couldn't…"

"Clara."

"Yes?"

"Do you want to wear one of these perfectly unobjectionable ball gowns to a Devil's Night?"

Clara sighed again. "No."

"Good. I knew you wouldn't disappoint. Come with me."

Clara did not know what she had expected from the bedchamber of a renowned courtesan. Cosmetics, gowns, silk chemises, and naughty sketches everywhere? Decanters of wine and brandy? But it was like any other room, with flower wallpaper and a chair with an embroidered cushion. A tea tray. Books by Plato and Aristotle.

Selene pulled a stunning gown from the armoire, red with a mesh overdress shining with brighter beads the color of rubies. The small sleeves dripped more beads. "It will be a little long on you," she warned.

"I do not have the bosom for that," Clara said regretfully. She'd never wanted to wear a dress more.

"We can adjust your stays for that, push them up until you rival even me." Selene glanced at her own spectacular cleavage, just in her chemise and dressing gown. "Well, maybe not *me*," she amended with a grin.

It seemed ridiculous to realize that Clara had never worn red, even as a child. Her mother would not have allowed it, and as she grew older, neither would Miss Vinegar.

"That plan of yours?" Selene pointed out. "You want them to underestimate you and overlook you. They won't do that if you wear one of your regular dresses ironically. Not tonight."

"I am tired of wearing white," Clara admitted. "Especially as I know it is unflattering."

"Who told you that?"

"My looking glass."

"You only needed a brighter shade and some color around your face, through your hair. But not tonight."

"Not tonight," she agreed.

Tonight she would wear red.

The dress made her feel different and yet herself. Her cheeks glowed; her lips were ripe with a hint of rouge. Selene would brook no protest.

She smiled smugly at her in the mirror. "I told you so."

"I… Thank you, Selene."

"You're very welcome."

Clara's smile died. "Be careful tonight."

"You too, Clara."

※

DEVIL'S NIGHT LIVED up to its name and reputation.

The enormous entrance hall was emptied of furniture and replaced with gaming tables and a huge, gilded cage where a woman dressed in feathers sat on a swing and blew kisses to the guests below. There was significantly more woman than feathers.

Candles burned in the crystal chandeliers above, and the oil lamps on the tables had all been replaced with red glass globes. Red roses, red tulips, red peonies, all burst from stone urns. Long tables were draped with red velvet and set with glass dishes and trays and china plates, exquisitely displaying strawberry cakes, currant wines, meringues dotted with rose petals. Red as far as the eye could see, until it tricked the viewer into considering they might truly have descended into some nether place.

The footmen were dressed in black, right down to their curled wigs accented with tiny horns, and they circled like silent shadows. The guests were in silks, velvets, rubies, garnets, cravats in every shade of crimson. Just like the food. And no mistake, they were here to be devoured as much as to devour.

The marquis had not forgone his customary blue coat, but it was embroidered in so much red it way as well have been the right color. He lounged with his entourage of fawning sycophants, laughing into his wine. No champagne tonight unless adorned with strawberries, making it looked stained with blood. He looked handsome, and well satisfied with himself.

Not like a man who had more than one woman hidden somewhere inside his fine house.

Clara wanted to punch him right in the eye.

"Steady," Bram said as if she had spoken out loud.

Devil stayed on the balcony, overseeing the proceedings, eyes sharp and deadly. He did not wear red, or a curled wig, only unrelieved black. His men circled below, armed, focused, and apparently untemptable.

The atmosphere hummed with expectation, fear, greed. Desperation, glamour, beauty. Clara had never seen anything like it. The very air tasted different in the back of her throat. Bram was at her side, wearing a dark burgundy coat and the same kind of watchful, vigilant expression Devil's men wore.

A hush immediately fell over the nearly two hundred guests when Devil moved to the railing. He did not even have to clear his throat or demand silence. It was given. An offering. Everything here had the feel of an offering.

"Welcome," he said. "You know the rules, but I will repeat them once and once only so that we are very, very clear. You can wager whatever you like, so long as you can follow through. Money, land deeds, inheritances, jewels. They all come due by sunrise. Vowels come to me and stay with me. Gaming is technically illegal, and debts cannot be enforced. Mine *can* and *will*. Ask the Duke of Wilmington what happens when you cross me."

Everyone knew about the duke. He, and the rest of the *ton*, had presumed he was untouchable. Dukes generally were. There was no rank above them that was not royal in nature, and indeed, many dukes also had royal blood. They had power, privilege. They could barely be accused, rarely punished, and never executed. aside from treason.

Devil had found a way to destroy him nonetheless.

The duke had tried to renege on a wager lost during a Devil's Night and paid the price. With interest. He lost his fortune, most of his houses, his mistresses, and his left foot. His was a tale whispered with fear in lavish drawing rooms and ballrooms dripping with gold.

Priya might be every bit as ruthless and clever, but she avoided notoriety. Devil did not. He used it like another weapon, just as sharp and wicked as any sword. Clara envied him that, just a little.

Time was running out, and she could not be subtle or covert any longer.

She would have to take a page from his book.

CHAPTER TWENTY-SIX

B Y ONE O'CLOCK in the morning, the marquis had lost a horse, three gold watches, and a house in Leeds. He had won Lady Susannah's coveted chef, and a mummy in a painted gold case arrived just recently from Cairo.

Two men had been thrown out for trying to strangle each other, and four duels were set for the next day. Four inheritances were lost on a single roll of a die. The laughter grew frenzied, interspersed with curses, sometimes weeping. Opera singers came and went, voices soaring to entertain and lend to the fantasy. The guests gambled and drank and ate, as if they had never been entertained a day in their lives. Billiard balls clacked loudly in the converted drawing room. Laughter reached a pitch that made Clara wince. This was not her milieu.

And yet...

She waited several hours, until her feet ached and she was thoroughly bored of the excess, before risking a card game. The round mahogany table, inset with red baize, seated several players: Lady Cabot, Lord Howell, two men she did not recognize, and the Marquis of Eastbourne.

Clara sat down. Lord Howell raised both eyebrows in her direction. "Are you sure?" he asked, not unkindly. When she nodded, he shrugged and went back to his port. The marquis barely acknowledged her. Bram closed his hand around the back of her chair as he had before, brushing her nape with his thumb. She took courage from that. More than was likely wise.

"The game is Brag," the dealer announced. "First ante."

Bets were placed: a gold watch, two diamond rings, a black pearl necklace. Clara bet the only thing of demonstrable value she had to her name: her father's sapphire cravat pin. It was ostentatious, flamboyant. Impossible to ignore. She felt a pang, but dismissed it. It did her more good here and now than in a jewelry box in her London townhouse, waiting to be sold for rent or food if her writing career was over.

One of the ladies complimented the diamond eye of the sapphire peacock. Lord Howell smiled at her. "I recognize that pin. It belonged to the Earl of Surrey."

Clara nodded. "My father."

"He did have singular taste."

She had to smile back. "Yes, he did."

The marquis won the first round, lounging back in his chair as though it were expected. Clara lost. Also expected. But at least she stayed in the game, whereas the two men she did not know folded entirely. She ignored the murmurs and the whispers. Two more rounds to go.

The marquis was smug and complacent and not entirely sober. No one was entirely sober, so that hardly signified. Save for Bram, of course, at attention and on duty. She couldn't tell him what she had planned. He would interfere with extreme prejudice.

And if it worked, he would absolutely murder her.

The second hand was dealt.

"I brag," the marquis said. Little surprise there.

Clara had a passable hand. She did not brag, but it kept her in the game. Lord Howell folded.

It was down to the marquis and Clara.

The marquis was more interested in the lady leaning on his arm, cleavage on great display. Clara could hardly blame him. The cleavage was impressive.

Selene had insisted on it.

She had dusted herself with a glimmering powder that smelled like sweet pastries, pasting a jewel just between the swells of her breasts. The result was impressive—and helpful. Not strictly cheating, and so not likely to be something Devil bothered with. If the marquis was so easily discombobulated by cleavage, he ought to close his eyes.

"I brag," he said again, eyes on Selene. She waved her fan, perfume softening the edges of the crowd.

"I brag," Clara returned, taking him by surprise. She bet her mother's favorite diamond bracelet.

And now she was officially out of items to bet.

Small problem—the game was not over.

The marquis frowned, annoyed. Before he could add anything to the wager, Clara cleared her throat. It was time to show her cards. Literally and figuratively.

The marquis was sweating, just a little. Selene waved her fan, three short waves, one flutter indicating that he did not have an unbeatable winning hand.

Clara had a chance.

Cheating did not bother her in the least when it came to abducted women. Devil might feel different. He was notoriously scrupulous about it. It was why Devil's Nights worked. A tiny, helpful nod from Selene was all they could risk.

"Shall we make this interesting, Lord Eastbourne?" Clara asked loudly.

He looked down his patrician nose at her. "We are already interesting, Lady Clara. Perhaps you are so little acquainted with the feeling that you fail to recognize it."

Where that might have cut her, just a little, some months ago, now it bored her. She yawned delicately beyond her fan. The insult did not go unnoticed. He bristled. "Anyone can wager money or jewels," she said. "I call a Clever Devil."

A Clever Devil was in no book on card games that she had ever read. It was only a quirk of Devil's Night. A trick to play before the last hand was revealed or the dice thrown. A wager on top of the wager, something unexpected. Unusual. Desperate.

"And what could you possibly have that *I* would want?" The marquis laughed. "You don't expect me to marry you, do you?"

More than one alliance had been wrought through a Clever Devil. Clara's answering laugh was unplanned and unstoppable. She would sooner marry a goat.

It was her laugh that did it.

A dowdy spinster disdaining a marquis. The crowd doubled in size. Wagers were placed behind them.

"What, then?" the marquis snapped.

Clara had no great fortune, no great beauty. Nothing to wager.

Except her own secret.

"I wager the identity of the Nightingale."

Eyes widened, and remarks rose like the tide. Someone scoffed. One of the guards looked up at Devil, who was still on the balcony, now directly overhead. He met Clara's gaze. She did not look away. Bram made a sound that could only be described as a warning growl.

The other risk to a Clever Devil was that if Devil did not approve it, the person calling for it lost the game immediately.

Clara held her breath.

"Clara," Bram said quietly, tense as a bowstring.

"Trust me," she whispered back. They had few options remaining. The party would be over soon and everyone would be expected to leave. They had to find Sybil and the others. Now. Tonight.

Devil inclined his head.

Wager accepted.

The marquis smirked, but there was a sharpness to it. She'd needled him publicly on purpose, poking his ego. Selene grabbed his arm excitedly. "How thrilling."

He glanced at her with condescending amusement. "She's hardly that famous, but very well. If you wish to meet her."

"You are too kind, my lord."

"And what is it you want from me?" he asked Clara. "Clearly, you have something in mind."

She smiled, prim and polite. "I should like Lady Heloise's thousand acres."

The marquis's smile slipped. "I beg your pardon?"

"Your ward, Lady Heloise. You control her fortune. I want her inheritance." The Spinsters worked with a very good solicitor who was adept at manipulating the law to make it work for women as best he could. He was quite feral about it. Clara would sign over Heloise's inheritance as soon as they returned to London. There were trusts, maneuvers. It wasn't foolproof, but it was something. It was better than nothing.

"Preposterous." The marquis laughed. "You can't be serious. I'm not betting that. What kind of a guardian would I be? I have a villa in Italy. I'll wager that instead."

He had already lost that villa. He was dreadful at cards and gambling, as it turned out. No wonder he was in debt.

Clara shrugged one shoulder. Plain, overlooked Clara in her daring red silk dress with matching red stocking ribbons. "I thought your parties were legendary. But if you're anxious..." She shrugged again, as disdainfully as she knew how. "If it's too rich for your blood..." She knew these people. She knew how they acted when there was blood in the water. She had been the prey long enough to learn their weaknesses.

He definitely noticed her now. Everyone did.

The good-natured ribbing started first. Then the jeers, the dares. She might have been in a schoolyard for all the finesse and self-control on display. But the marquis, while placated daily, was also resented. He was careless and self-centered. More important-ly, he was above almost every single person here in terms of rank and fortune. They wanted to see him fall. Just once. From such a great height.

She'd counted on it.

She had been invisible for so long, but now it was time to be seen. He needed to notice her, and there was no catching his attention without fortune or beauty. Unless it was with rage. Humiliation.

A dangerous game, but necessary. A red dress was not enough.

She waited quietly but allowed herself a toss of the single curl Selene had arranged over her shoulder. A reach for her wine glass, set so near his own. A tip of her hand.

Gauntlet thrown.

The marquis glared at her then smiled that careless, indolent smile. "I did promise entertainment," he announced, as though this was all his idea. She would let him have that if he agreed to the terms. The marquis gave a great, theatrical sigh. "I suppose, if only to indulge the ladies," he said. "I accept your terms."

Clara fought to conceal the thrill of the first triumph.

If you could call it that. Because if she lost…

No. It wasn't helpful to dwell on that now. There was no going back. Bram was so still and so alert behind her that it felt as though a coiled panther waited at her shoulder. The marquis flicked him a glance.

"We should clear the floor behind each player, don't you think?" she asked. "So there is no concern over cheating?"

Cheating was not her worry. For her backup to work, Bram could not be within arm's reach of her. The dealer glanced at Devil, who nodded again, thoughtfully. His men ushered the spectators to the sides, clearing the space behind the marquis and Clara.

Bram cursed under his breath. "Clara."

She only smiled at him. He grumbled, finally stepping aside.

The marquis studied her face, trying to read her expression, but she had years of training in this particular field. He would see only what she allowed him to see: proper, plain Miss Vinegar, in over her head. Yes, the very one who did not recognize entertainment. Until it was too late.

The marquis's hand was very good.

Hers was better.

He hissed a curse. Someone gasped as though they were at the theatre. Clara did not preen, though she dearly wanted to.

Very well, she preened *a little*. For the plan, of course. Not her own *entertainment*.

"The lady wins," the dealer announced over the general commotion.

"Absurd," the marquis bit out, temper flaring.

"The terms were set," Devil said coldly from above them. The shadows hid his eyes, but his tone was clear enough. "You have until sunrise, Eastbourne, to bring me the papers." A faint smile. "Well done, Lady Clara."

Clara gathered her peacock pin and her diamond bracelet and the rest of her winnings, stuffing them into her reticule. It gave her the opportunity to make sure her other supplies were at hand. The spectators crowded in as the marquis made his displeasure known. Clara used the confusion of bodies and fans and elbows to slip further into the crowd.

Away from Bram.

"Clara!"

CHAPTER TWENTY-SEVEN

CLARA HEARD BRAM shout her name and did not turn back, did not dare to even pause.

She could not afford to talk herself out of this mad plan. They had run out of time and options. Winning Heloise's fortune did not do Heloise any good if they could not find her.

And Clara was certain they were here.

The mistakenly delivered trays, the secret passageway, the keys, the doves, the fact that Sybil had not made it to the next town.

And so Clara kept on, fleeing in her red dress, between the red frock coats, the red shawls, the red velvet tablecloths. She could lose herself, just for a moment. Just long enough.

There was movement behind her, someone scuffling with someone else. Bram was closing in; he must be. She ducked out of the main room, through the nearest billiards room, and down a hall lit with sconces. The sound of footsteps behind her. Not Bram.

A hand gripped her shoulder hard and dragged her around. One of the marquis's men dressed as a footman. "You're coming with us."

"Unhand me." Too much? Not enough. "How dare you."

"Hurry up," another footman snapped, hurrying their way. "Before that big ox of hers finds us."

The grip on her bare shoulder was purposely too forceful. Clara's misgivings turned into fear. She made sure they saw it, though it stung her pride.

As he dragged her down the hall, she struggled, scratching, flailing her limbs wildly, mostly to cover the fact that she had dug into her reticule. They took her down the stairs at the end of the hallway, where she dropped a red ribbon on the top step.

Through a forgotten door, out into the kitchen garden, where no one wandered at this hour.

Through the hedges, along the garden wall, past the door with the orchid.

Another red ribbon on a branch.

To another door set behind a tangle of lilac bushes.

Red ribbon, red ribbon. She scattered them like lampposts along St. James, pointing the way to the best clubs. All the way into the grotto, away from the flickering candlelight and the sounds of music and laughter from those enjoying alternate amusements, down to another warren of caves much less frequented. There were no statues here, no glass lamps, no tapestries to soften the damp.

Only stone and metal locks and a room filled with missing women.

⇶⫷

WHEN BRAM SAW Clara's pale hair vanish into the crowd, he bellowed her name. The guests nearby stared at him, drawing back. Not fast enough, not nearly fast enough.

She was gone. She had taunted the bloody marquis on purpose, and now she was gone.

Fury and panic warred inside his ribcage, but he could give in to neither, no matter how desperately he wanted to start overturning gaming tables and punching footmen until someone told him where she was. The marquis was amusing his guests, pretending that there was not an edge to his laugh, that he had not been manipulated by a woman no one bothered to notice.

Bram would start punching there. With great relish. Followed by tearing the marquis limb from limb if necessary.

A whistle from the balcony above. He glanced up out of instinct.

Devil, leaning indolently on the railing as though Bram's life hadn't just exploded, nodded toward the far doorway. It opened onto the hall that led past the billiards rooms to the conservatory and the gardens. Bram didn't bother nodding back, just shoved through the sea of chattering aristocrats. It was all a game to them, the whole evening, their entire lives.

Clara would not pay the price.

He barreled out of the doors, noticing the flowers in one of the urns had been snapped. Nothing else was disturbed. No one lingered.

That was when he saw the tiny scrap of red ribbon by his boot. He knew that silk well, had had dreams of pulling it off with his teeth. Clever, clever woman.

When he reached down to grab it, the blow came from behind, smashing against the back of his skull.

"THIS IS NOT quite the rescue I had in mind."

The cave was rough, damp, the chill barely softened by a battalion of candles. Clara would have preferred an army of actual soldiers ready to do her bidding.

Heavy, old-fashioned furniture of the sort generally brought down from family attics was scattered about: chairs, a long table, books, and baskets of needlework, all under a narrow window too small to fit through and barred with iron. There were several mattresses behind moth-eaten tapestries attached to the ceiling.

And Sybil, also attached, though to the wall.

She was the only one in chains, which made sense. She would have been the one to cause the most trouble. "Hello, Clara," she added.

Clara had been shoved inside the room, hitting the hard ground on her knees. The thick wooden door shut with an ominous thud, followed by the sharp clack of the lock turning. When she looked up, Sybil smiled wryly. Clara sat back, dusting off her hands. "Found you."

"Lucky you."

"Quite." Pretending to be calm was helping her feel calmer. As was the knowledge that Bram would find them. It sat in her ribcage as surely as her heart did. "Finally, my own adventure."

"And is it everything you dreamed of?"

One of the ladies huddled together in the far corner stepped closer. She wore several shawls over her dress. She was very short, with a forceful nose and serious eyes. "Why isn't she fainting?" she asked Sybil. "Or screaming?"

"Lady Heloise, this is Lady Clara. Lady Rosalinde and Miss Blanche Yarwood just there."

"A pleasure. And I'm a Spinster, dear," Clara added briskly, climbing to her feet. Her knees were definitely bruised, and the left one did not seem at all interested in supporting her weight. "We don't give in to histrionics."

However much she might want to.

Heloise snorted. "Sybil tore up the tapestries and then tried to strangle one of the guards within an hour of our being imprisoned."

"That's not histrionics," Sybil said. "That's just good sense."

"It landed you in chains," Heloise pointed out.

"A momentary setback," Sybil assured her. She looked to Clara. "Took you long enough to figure out my clues."

"Because they were haphazard and half mad," Clara replied. "Until I found your letter, they were not particularly helpful."

"I couldn't risk anything falling into the marquis's hands."

"I understand that now. There were rather a lot of keys."

"I started collecting them as soon as I realized we were being locked in the attic at night. I knew something was definitely off. I didn't know where we might need to get into, or out of. And there are too many locked doors in this house. It's not natural."

"Why exactly did you leave me keys to the sex grotto?"

"There's a sex grotto?" Sybil asked. "I had no idea. I was just trying to unlock doors."

Clara looked around. Rosalinde was slightly wild eyed, her dark hair wound into a crown braid. Blanche was tall, with blonde curls and an upturned nose. "Is anyone hurt? Miss Yarwood, your fever?"

"I never had a fever."

"No, I thought not."

"I managed to get away early one morning, but they caught me in the village. They told everyone I was plagued by a fever and rambling nonsense."

"Physically, we are fine," Sybil assured Clara. "Meals delivered on a regular basis, even tea to drink."

"Plain scones and no butter," Clara said. "I knew that tray came to us accidentally."

"You found me because the scones were not up to your standards?"

"Yes."

"Clara, I don't say this very often, but you are my favorite Spinster. Don't tell Peony."

Clara smiled faintly, then lowered her voice. "Is everyone truly well?"

"Well enough, all things considered. Rosalinde has been here the longest, nearly eight months? Nine, maybe? She will need care, I think, but I have every confidence in her ability to recover."

"I'll be fine once I can get warm again," Rosalinde muttered, sitting on the edge of one of the mattresses. She was thin and pale, lips faintly blue, smudges under her eyes.

"And she has very good hearing," Sybil pointed out.

"Our prison is not exactly spacious," Rosalinde said.

"True enough."

"Will you tell us what's happening out there?" Blanche asked. "I thought I heard music."

"It's Devil's Night," Clara told her. "The Hall is full of gambling and wine, and the caves are full of…other things."

"So no one will hear us," Blanche said. "I've been screaming through that little window for hours."

"It has not been at all vexing to the nerves," Sybil said.

"You have no nerves," Clara reminded her.

"Oh, right."

Clara inspected her chains, the reddened, raw skin around Sybil's ankle. "Oh, Sybil."

"It could be much worse," Sybil said. There were shadows under her eyes as well, despite her bravado. "I am just cross I let myself get taken. I was meant to protect Heloise."

"You tried," Heloise said. "Harder than some of my own family."

"We're not beaten," Clara said. "Not yet."

"Easy for you to say—you're still warm and clean. What about Martin?" Heloise asked. "Is he… How is he?"

"He is fine," Clara assured her. "Though he did try to stab the marquis when you did not show up at the inn. It was not very covertly done."

"Bloody footmen caught us halfway there," Sybil said, scowling. "The marquis stationed them on both roads leading away from the Hall. I think he suspected me long before I realized it, which is galling to admit, I don't mind telling you."

"Martin really tried to stab someone?" Heloise asked.

"Twice," Clara said. "Luckily, he is not very good at murder."

"Who else did he attack?" Sybil asked.

"Bram."

"Captain Thorn?" Sybil's eyes widened. "And he lived to tell the tale?"

"He did."

"Wait, Bram is really here with you?"

Clara nodded. "I'm sure he'll be along any moment now."

"I'm not criticizing your plan, Clara," Sybil said, "but waiting for rescue is not…comfortable. Believe me, I know. And how do *you* know he will find us?"

"I let myself be taken on purpose," Clara explained, before telling them about the wager. "And then I left a trail for him to follow. He would never have agreed otherwise, and we were running out of time."

Heloise stared at her. "You risked yourself for me? You truly won my inheritance back?" A shadow passed over her face. "It's not legal, though, is it? Not really?"

"We have a very clever and very feral lawyer," Clara told her. "And I am not entirely unarmed, by the way."

She pulled a dagger, three uncomfortable hatpins, and a packet of herbs from inside her stays. Her poison ring was now empty.

"And now you have Devil on your side," she added. "There's no one more fearsome in England. And he always enforces his wagers. Always."

"Brilliant, Clara," Sybil said. "Devil is better than Parliament and the House of Lords in these cases," she explained to the others. "And the entire army."

Clara glanced at the locked door. "And you've never met Captain Thorn."

⟫⟫⟫⟪⟪⟪

CAPTAIN THORN WAS currently occupied with regaining his consciousness at the bottom of the stairs.

He woke with more blood on him than he remembered bleeding when he fell. Struck from behind. Cowardly blighter. There would be a reckoning.

He sat up, groaning as pain throbbed through his skull. His hand came away wet with blood, but it was already thickening.

Head wounds looked like slaughter even when they weren't. His bones protested every movement.

He was too damned old to get thrown down the stairs.

But he was not about to let it stop him. There was a piece of red silk in his fist, wet with his blood. *Clara.*

His first step was more of a stagger. He cursed, low and filthy, and cautiously moved forward, hunting for more clues, watching for ambushes.

He found another red ribbon.

The house behind him fair thrummed with sound and light, hundreds of candles burning as hundreds of people caroused. It was just past three in the morning, but you'd never know it. He wouldn't be the only one with a sore head tomorrow, and not just because he planned to bash a few in.

He'd been in the middle of the sea when his baby sister needed him and was unable to get to her. He'd been *right bloody there* when Clara needed him. Like hell would anything stop him from getting to her. Not now, not ever.

The stone path took him around the side of the grotto. He'd searched the house and the caves to no avail. It took him some time to find the ribbon stuck in the lilac thicket, just by the hidden door. Time he did not have.

He had to use even more precious seconds moving carefully, both because his vision went double and because he did not want to give any guard posted below too much forewarning. He was enraged enough to take on all comers, but even he might have trouble dodging a musket ball in a corridor, righteous fury or not.

The first guard was unconscious before he hit the ground. Bram grabbed him from behind and tossed him into the wall, headfirst. He was still sliding down the damp stones when Bram stepped over him. Two more men waited at the bottom of another set of moss-slick stairs. One of them leapt to his feet. Bram was gratified to see neither had a musket or a pistol.

Idjits.

He charged, fear and fury propelling him forward. They

stood between him and Clara.

They would not stand for much longer.

He met the first guard with a punch to the gut. He choked and stumbled back. His companion was next and nearly as wide as Bram. He cracked Bram in the eye, shaking the rest of his brains loose in his skull. Fortunately, it seemed to shake his vision back to normal as well.

The candles flickered as they fought, throwing shadows, playing tricks. Bram took a glancing blow to the ribs and retaliated with a crack to the man's jaw. It echoed through the hall, bouncing off the stones. As did his groan of pain. Blood spattered the walls.

Three more hits to jaw, gut, and nose and the second guard fell, eyes rolling back. Bram crouched, rifling through his pockets for the key. When he jammed it into the lock, the man groaned, shifted to stop him. Bram used him as a battering ram and threw him straight into the cave. He landed in a bloody heap at Clara's feet.

"Why, thank you, Captain Thorn. What a thoughtful gift."

CHAPTER TWENTY-EIGHT

C LARA DID NOT give the injured heap of a man at her feet a second glance.

All she saw was Bram.

Steady as a stone, blood in his hair, and bruises on his face. His eyes were savage. They searched her carefully, looking for injuries. She saw the exact moment he noticed the reddening marks on her shoulder. His jaw clenched. "Did he do that to you?"

"One of them did. I'm not sure which."

"Then they'll each pay."

She stepped over the sprawled guard to touch her fingertips lightly to his face. "You're hurt."

"I'm fine."

"Then I am too."

"You're limping," he roared.

Sybil rattled her chains. Loudly. "As romantic as I am sure this all is, I would dearly love to regain feeling in my left foot. And that cretin there has the key in his right coat pocket."

Bram looked over Clara's shoulder. "Hello, Miss Taunton."

"Captain Thorn, how do you do?"

Clara bent to retrieve the key, but Bram stopped her. "Don't."

"He's unconscious."

"I'll trust this lot when they're dead, and not a moment before." He fished it out of the right pocket himself and handed it to Clara. "I'll get the other one. They can rot in here, in the dark, until someone can be bothered to come get them." He turned to Heloise, Blanche, and Rosalinde. "Ladies, right this way."

Heloise marched out like a very short, enraged general as Clara unlocked Sybil. Blanche followed. Rosalinde hesitated. "It's all right," Sybil said softly. "No one will ever get to you again. Certainly not the marquis."

Rosalinde nodded mutely.

"Do you remember I told you about my friend Peony? I thought they would send her—no offense to you, Clara."

"None taken," Clara sighed.

"Offense very much taken," Bram grumbled, dragging in the guard from the hall. Blood was drying on the back of his collar.

"Anyway," Sybil continued, "Peony will teach you to stab a man and how to run so fast he chokes on his own lungs before catching you. And if that's not enough, you're going to be very rich again, very soon. You can hire as many bodyguards as you like."

Rosalinde nodded again, more confidently.

Bram blew out the candles before locking the guards inside the cave. There was a shout of alarm from within. He ignored it. "You're going to have to hide while we corner the marquis."

"What about the dower house?" Clara suggested. "Just for a little while. We need to make this public. He wants it hidden away, so we shine every light on it."

Sybil smiled grimly. "Oh, do let me help."

"We are all helping," Rosalinde said forcefully, though she trembled.

"She's right." Blanche took her hand.

"Only we can keep him properly distracted," Sybil agreed. "While you get the evidence, Clara. Do you have the key?"

"I have them all," Clara replied.

"Good. You need to bring us the box that's hidden in his

private study. It's letters mostly, and although it might not be enough, it's a start."

"You hid it in his own study?"

"I hid it in the very last place he would ever think to look. Under his own feet."

"Mad. Brilliant, but also mad."

"You'd be surprised how many times I have heard that said."

"I don't think I would, actually."

"Are you two quite finished bantering?" Heloise asked. "I should like my pound of flesh now, if you please."

⟫⟫⟫⟪⟪⟪

A QUARTER OF an hour later, Clara and Bram stood outside the main hall for just a moment, watching Sybil, Heloise, Blanche, and Rosalinde advance on the marquis from every corner of the glittering room, like a chorus of Furies.

Methodically, patiently. Lionesses in faded and worn dresses, pale from the lack of sunlight, thin from imprisonment. And all the more fierce for it.

They were the only ones not dressed in red, not dripping pearls and diamonds. The only ones garnering any attention at all and holding it, effortlessly.

Past the billiards room, the marquis's study was not guarded. Bram frowned but did not say anything. There was still blood in his hair, on his temple. On his knuckles. Clara knew he was angry with her, but she also knew he would never let it interfere with his duties. Or with her safety.

While the door was unguarded, it was also locked.

Luckily, this time, Clara was sure she had the right key, as they did not have time to pick the lock. She pulled her necklace free, trying them all until one fit.

"I don't like it," he muttered as they slipped inside. "That was too easy. And there are too many fronts in his battle."

"You said yourself his arrogance knows no limits."

"But now he also knows you know enough about Heloise to use her in a wager."

Fair point.

Too late now.

An oil lamp burned low inside the study, set on the edge of the window seat so the glass reflected it and nothing else. Clara hurried to the fireplace, the floor creaking under her feet as she pulled back the hand-knotted rug. Underneath, nothing to indicate there was anything suspicious. Clara looked up, searching for the tiny blue dove she now knew hovered overhead. Sybil would have left a sign. "To your left," Bram said. "By the chandelier."

She spotted it, followed the line of sight down to the correct floorboard, and pressed on the corner. A bit more force and it budged. A bit more and it flipped open like the lid of a particularly large box.

Underneath was a bundle of blue cloth, unmistakably cut from one of the marquis's famous coats. Inside, folded letters. Evidence.

"We've got it," Clara said excitedly.

It was not Bram who answered.

"The marquis sends his thanks."

Bram cursed when the cold metal of a pistol touched his bloody temple.

"You must have a skull made of stone," the footman said.

"Let her go," Bram replied, "and you might survive the night."

"I told you those stairs weren't enough to do him in," the second footman complained.

"Shut up, we've got him now."

Clara had stopped breathing at some point during the exchange. All she could see was the pistol pressing into Bram's skin. She felt ill. Furious. Terrified.

"Clara, look at me," he said quietly. His eyes were so blue. So calm. He was about to be shot, and he was comforting *her*.

She straightened her spine. He smiled briefly.

"Hand us those papers there," the second footman demanded, "and maybe we won't kill him."

"Don't," Bram said. "He'll kill me either way."

Clara was a woman who used rules and decorum and laudanum in tea poured in the proper way. She wasn't a woman who knew the first thing about guns or fighting. She wasn't Sybil, or Peony.

She was Miss Vinegar.

And she'd forgotten her own lessons.

Her posture wilted. Her eyelids fluttered.

Bram's gaze sharpened.

"Hand it here," the footman barked.

He did not expect her to fight. He did not expect anything from her at all, beyond a certain measure of fear and compliance. And as she had told Miss Cunningham what felt like months ago: if you gave people what they expected, they seldom looked any deeper.

So she would give them exactly what they expected.

"I feel…" She let herself collapse, the papers still firmly in hand. It was just a moment of distraction.

It was all Bram needed.

Before she hit the floor, he had the footman disarmed. A step backward out of the trajectory of the bullet, a hard hit to the other man's forearm, and the pistol dropped into Bram's waiting palm. He followed it with a powerful punch, breaking the man's nose. The crack sounded through the library.

The second footman lunged forward. Clara kicked out, catching him in the ankles.

He toppled like a startled tree. His head bounced off the raised floorboard and he rolled over, groaning. Bram punched the first footman, now clutching his bleeding face, in the nose again. He gave a howl that turned to a gurgle of pain and doubled over, but not before he managed to pull the bell cord. The tassel was blue and gold and did not look like the regular summons for household staff.

"I don't think that calls for a tea tray," Bram said, pulling Clara to her feet. "You're going to be the death of me, woman."

"You're welcome," she said tartly. Elation and vindication coursed through her like champagne.

Too many charging footsteps sounded in the corridor.

Bram took her hand. "Time to go."

CHAPTER TWENTY-NINE

THERE WAS NOWHERE to go.

The hall was filling with the marquis's men. There was no time to crawl out of the window, no armoire to hide in.

But there was a secret passageway in the house.

It might end in a locked door, but Clara was now in possession of a great many keys.

Bram dragged a table in front of the door and lodged it under the handle. It would buy them a few minutes. Hopefully it would be enough.

"What are the odds that the marquis has a secret passageway that he can access from his personal study?"

"The odds? You're the gambler, you tell me."

"The odds are extremely good," she replied. He was already searching the study, pulling on candleholders and feeling for odd spaces between bookshelves, books that did not quite fit. The wooden paneling extended along the back wall, heavy with scrollwork and carvings, confusing to the eye. Swans flew over leaping deer.

The handle rattled and there was cursing from the hall.

Clara pushed at each panel, guided mostly by instinct—and the fact that they had checked everything else, down to the painted globe on the mantel. Nothing else had worked. "Please," she muttered. "Please, please."

"There," Bram said suddenly. He reached over her and used his considerable strength to push. A click, a puff of musty air. He shoved harder and the door opened. Clara stumbled into her darkness, Bram at her back. He hauled the paneled door shut behind them.

Darkness swallowed them.

"I'm not sure this is an improvement," Clara said.

"I have a tinder box," Bram said. She heard him open the little box, the strike of flint, and the hiss of the char cloth catching. A tiny flame sputtered. "There's bound to be a candle or something nearby," he said, lighting the sulfur-tipped matchstick. "The marquis would not stumble about in the dark."

She felt around until she found a rush light. Bram had it burning before she could wipe the dirt from her gloves. "This time you go first," he said, holding it high. "Just in case they find the same door behind us."

The corridor was narrow, with hanging cobwebs that fluttered as they passed. She used to the scent of lime candies through the musty damp to steady her. Her heart raced, making her feel lightheaded. They were so close.

Voyeur holes spied into the drawing room where the revelers were draped over each other, smoking opium pipes as they watched dancing girls. The corridor branched off to the familiar hall they had first discovered, the locked door.

"If we can get through here, it'll bring us out closer to where we need to come out," Bram said.

Clara tried her new keys. The first did not work.

The second opened the lock, if with slight protest. "Finally," she muttered.

Bram would not let her push the door open, expecting tricks and traps. He was a very suspicious man.

Also a very wise man.

The snick of the crossbow was the only warning before the bolt flew past his nose. Clara squeaked, grabbing the back of his coat. "Don't move," he warned.

Clara remained still except for her heart, which was galloping throughout her body.

"That paranoid bawbag. I hit the tripwire with my boot. Wonder what else he's bloody hiding. Clara, I daren't move. I don't know what other traps he might have set. Take the tin of candies from my inside pocket," he said calmly. "Carefully. Reach from behind."

Clara pulled his coat back, sneaking her hand up and digging her fingers into the lining of the fabric. She found the tin.

"Good," he said. "Now toss a candy forward, about head height."

She did as he asked.

Another crossbow bolt was immediately triggered. Had Bram stepped forward even an inch, it would have gone through his neck. She shuddered.

"Someone needs to break his bloody jaw," he muttered.

Inside the hidden chamber was a table with a ledger and a stack of papers, a chair, several boxes, and a trunk. They finally understood why the key worked in the door leading outside to the hall but it still would not open. It was barricaded from the inside.

"Toss another one."

By the third candy, nothing else came flying at them from the walls. No bolts or arrows or rusty medieval swords.

"Are there more traps, do you think?" Clara asked. The candlelight was not quite bright enough to reach the corners. Who knew what lurked in those shadows?

"I'd bet on it," Bram said.

"I think I'm wagered out for the night," she returned.

"I need something else to toss, preferably round. I want to test the floor."

"I'm all out of cannonballs. I might be able to jump onto the table from here?"

"Like hell. Find me something, pirate."

She searched the ground behind them, but there were no

convenient stones or rubble. Nothing on her person. Nothing else in Bram's pockets. She studied the floor. "We only need a bit more light," Clara said.

"How do you reckon?"

"I highly doubt the marquis dusts the place himself, and he definitely doesn't have the housemaids in to do it," she said. "We should be able to see the stones that haven't been disturbed by footprints and avoid those, just in case."

"Clever lass," Bram said.

"A spinster must learn to keep house and supervise the staff," she said with a pretend sniff. "Page twenty-seven of *The Manners and Morals of A Virtuous Woman*."

"I will never mock her again."

"You should—she's deadly dull."

Bram found an oil lamp just inside the door. "Here we are." He lit the wick, and the warm glow suffused the room. It had been a parlor once, still decorated for someone to sit in a soft chair with their favorite book. There was a faded mural on the ceiling full of angels and violent clouds. The floor would have been polished parquet once upon a time, but it was now very helpfully dusty. It was simple enough to follow the footsteps to the desk.

Clara trailed after Bram, peering carefully at every floorboard. "Do you really think there are traps?"

"False floorboards falling away into a pit, stakes, any number of ways to maim a person."

"I'll have to use that in one of my books."

"What was that?" he asked, turning around to make sure she was safely stepping exactly where he had stepped.

"Nothing," she said hastily. "Let's see what he's hiding in this letter box here."

This box held more than correspondence from frantic friends and families.

There were also lists of women who stood to inherit should a single parent or guardian meet their early demise.

At the marquis's hand.

Their fortunes were listed in great detail, the names of relatives, any secrets they might have. Magistrates in the area who might be bought off. As well as a collection of women's jewelry, which no doubt had gone missing the moment they arrived at the Hall: necklaces, ear bobs, tiaras.

Heloise, Blanche, Rosalinde. And five other names Clara did not recognize. Those ladies could be anywhere. If they were even still alive.

And there was another ledger documenting the staggering amount of debt the marquis owed in lost wagers.

"Right. Let's send this bastard to hell." Bram hefted up the heavy box. "After you."

They stumbled into the sea of red ball gowns and cravats, of rubies and diamonds, covered in dust and blood.

It wasn't quite as dramatic an entrance as Sybil and the others, but it did the trick.

Guests moved out of the way before Bram even had a chance to snap out an order, or shove a dandy into the punch bowl. The marquis was surrounded by four enraged women, inside a circle of curious guests, and his footmen, armed to the teeth. Devil's men closed in.

Clara held up the papers, slightly crumpled. "I have the evidence."

"Letters from Miss Yarwood's solicitors in Wales," Sybil said. "Accusations supported by Lady Rosalinde's village in Ireland, including two vicars and a bishop. Lady Heloise's estate manager and the marquis's own solicitor offer proof. He selected women with large inheritances who lived too far away to have any nearby ties, any recourses. And then he convinced or threatened their families until he was granted guardianship. After which he locked his new wards in the caves underneath the house."

"Don't be absurd!" The marquis laughed, but Clara fancied she could hear a frisson of trepidation to it. He liked to laugh when he was cornered. As a woman who liked to lecture on the most mind-numbingly dull points of decorum when she was cornered, Clara was not fooled.

"As well as very careful lists of these women and others, with their fortunes and family members," Clara added. "Which he hid inside the walls. Five more women who should be searched for."

"You did this to us," Blanche said. "To all of us."

"You're still unwell," the marquis added with a shake of his head, gently concerned. "That fever. And Heloise was sent to the seaside." A sharp glance at his footmen, the ones who would not know a champagne coupe from a pudding bowl. "I left her in the capable hands of a chaperone. We've all been deceived, clearly. Poor darlings."

"Miss Taunton was not the one who locked me in the caves beneath the house," Heloise said firmly.

"Nor I," added Blanche.

"Nor I." This from Rosalinde in surprisingly ringing tones. "You murdered my grandfather, didn't you?"

The crowd was turning—even the marquis could sense it. They were riveted, suspicious.

The marquis's gaze, full of hatred and rage, fell on Clara and her letters. "I'll kill you, you little bitch."

Bram stepped in front of her, seething and raw with the kind of power the marquis could only dream of. "Fucking try it."

There was no pretending he was not able and willing to rip a man to pieces, lord or not. A flutter of warmth went through Clara. Perhaps she ought to be appalled.

She most definitely was not.

But nor was she going to let Bram be deported or hanged for attacking a marquis.

It could too easily spiral out of control. People would be hurt, maybe killed. The story would become focused on Devil's Night, on the violence, and not the accusations. Not the *consequences*. The marquis would get away. It wouldn't be about Heloise, Blanche, or Rosalinde. Or the other women. Their justice would fall to the wayside.

No.

"One moment, if you please," Clara cut in, in her best, sharpest governess tones.

It was the command of a spinster who lived in a cottage by the sea and spent her days painting watercolors of cows and crocheting doilies. Who knew the lineage of every passing peer in the village. Who read *Four Diocese Sermons* for fun and wore prim, boring dresses. Who gave out copies of *The Manners and Morals of the Virtuous Woman* every Christmas.

And it was so distinctly out of place that everyone paused.

Even the marquis turned his head slowly to blink at her blearily.

And then his eyes rolled back in his head, and he fainted, rather like a spinster shocked by the brazen behavior of the younger set.

Even Devil's men were nonplussed, frozen with their weapons still raised.

"It's the laudanum," Clara explained. "It can take some time to take effect, I'm afraid—if you are accustomed to a higher dose." She grinned back at Bram, who was smiling at her even though he still stood as though he was ready to run people through. "I had to guess."

"Pirate," he said softly, fondly. He glanced up at Devil. "You know he was going to renege. He's already up to his ass in debts. He hasn't got half of what he lost here tonight."

"Obviously," Devil replied.

"Can you send your men for a magistrate? I assume you have one available for…complications."

"I do." He nodded to one of his men, who immediately headed out into the night. With one more nod, his men closed in, muscling aside the footmen who suddenly hovered like marionettes with no one to man the strings.

"You may wait in the cloakroom for the magistrate," Clara told them sharply.

She had to hide her surprise when they obeyed. Devil's men

at their backs were no doubt incentive enough. "Well done, Lady Clara," Devil said smoothly, impressed.

Bram snorted. "Get your own spinster."

Everyone agreed it was the best house party the marquis had ever hosted.

The best party of the decade, in fact.

Even if he did end up in chains in his own cellar before dawn.

Maybe *especially* because he ended up in chain in his own cellar before dawn.

Bram was not inclined to be merciful. Devil did not know how to be. Clara had a feeling that the marquis only survived the sunrise because there were too many witnesses.

⇥⟫⟫⟫⟪⟪⟪⇤

CLARA WAS BACK in her bedroom, the sun washing the sky with pink and orange, with a package wrapped in pretty blue and gold paper waiting for her on the bed. Across it had been written: *A gift courtesy of the Marquis of Eastbourne.*

A copy of her new book. Care of Kitty and the Golden Griffin Bookshop, no doubt, before the night had taken such a turn.

"Everyone got one," Bram said from the doorway. "Nightingale's new book, delivered during the festivities. Hell of a party favor, if you'll pardon the pun."

That was when Clara realized she had never made it to the lion fountain.

Not that she had five thousand pounds to pay the blackmail in any case. But she'd planned to lie in wait, hopefully catch a glimpse. Find out who had been sending her those notes. Punch them at least once, very hard, right in the nose.

"What is it?" Bram asked, watching her carefully. "Do you need something? Tea? Whiskey? A basket of scones? Mrs. Meadows already sent one up with six different types of marmalade."

She shook her head. "I'm fine. Better than fine. Sybil and the others are safe."

They were sleeping in Devil's suite of rooms, as he would be leaving right after breakfast. Apparently, he never lingered. Heloise had run down to the cottage, to see if Martin waited for her. As she had not returned, she had clearly found him. A message confirming it had arrived shortly after dawn.

"But?" Bram prodded.

Clara busied herself with pouring water from the pitcher into the basin and fetching a towel. "You still have blood in your hair."

"But?" Bram repeated, not moving.

"I didn't get a chance to corner my blackmailer," she admitted. Satisfied, he shut the door behind him and stalked toward her. It was like being cornered by a giant Viking. Delicious.

"Sit down," she ordered him primly, instead of jumping on him like she wanted to. The man must have the very devil of a headache.

He sat down. "The bawbag never showed for his payment," he said, nodding to the book.

"How do you know that?"

"I had someone watching."

"You did? Why didn't you tell me?"

"Because I knew you were up to something," he replied, grunting when she wiped his bruises and bumps gently. She eased him out of his shirt to wash the back of his neck and muscular shoulders. "And I was right, wasn't I? Provoking the marquis like that."

"It worked."

"You took ten years off my life."

"You're the one who was beaten and held at gunpoint." Her voice trembled, despite her brisk and efficient nursing. The events of the night were catching up to her. All the ways it could all have gone horribly wrong.

He touched her wrists, stilling her until she met his gaze. "I'm perfectly fine."

"There's blood all over you."

"It'll wash off."

"Your head must ache."

"Not for the first time, and not the last."

She scowled. "Stop being so reasonable. I want to march right back to the cloakroom and smash things over those footmen's heads. Heavy things."

He moved his hand up her arm, clasping the back of her neck, angling her head back for his kiss. It was deep and stirring, a claiming. She sighed into his mouth, and he pulled her closer, settling her between his sturdy thighs, pinning her there. His tongue stroked, tangled, tasted. Heat pooled in the center of her. His big hands gripped her hair, her hips. He was taking everything: her breath, her desires, her worries. All that was left was want and need. When he finally pulled away, they were both panting.

"I'm not letting you out of my sight now, pirate."

"Won't the magistrate or the others need you?"

"You need me," he said as if that was all there was to it.

She took his hand and led him to the bed as the morning light pierced the clouds and gilded the treetops, finally reaching the gold thread of the coverlet. Water dripped from Bram's hair and ran between the tattooed swallows on his bare chest. He pulled her down to the mattress, dragging his mouth under her ear and down over her breasts, sucking lightly at her nipples. She was already wet for him, pulling him closer, exhausted by the evening's events but trembling with energy.

They rode each hard, mercilessly. Desperately. He refused to give in until her pleasure claimed her, and their gasps rang out together, like music.

SEVERAL HOURS LATER, Clara bolted awake.

She recognized the handwriting on the paper-wrapped copy of her new book.

She knew it was familiar, but there had been too much to sort through for her mind to catch up to the uneasy pit in her stomach.

She dressed quickly, taking in the sight of Bram sprawled naked in her bed the entire time she fussed with her stays and her dress. A warm mountain of a man who wore his story in the scars and ink across his body. She desperately wanted to crawl back under the covers and curl into him. For the rest of the day. The week. The entire year. They could eat nothing but scones and tea while they devoured each other.

Instead, Clara marched down the stairs, bleary with lack of sleep and aching all over with time better spent in her bed. There was beard prickle on the inside of one thigh and faint pink marks on her throat, hidden by a wide ribbon. Red, naturally.

Selene was in the parlor, drinking coffee. A huge tray piled with half the food in the kitchens sat next to her. Bram had not exaggerated. There were at least four different types of scones and more marmalade than any family could safely consume in a week.

"The strawberry rose jam is my favorite," Selene said, putting down her copy of the newest Nightingale book. Blue and gold paper was folded neatly on the table. "Mrs. Meadows even spoke directly to me directly this morning," she added. "That's thanks to you."

Clara shook her head. "She knows what you did to help us stop the marquis."

Selene shrugged. "I don't usually bother much with people's opinions of me, but I've been trying to crack that old chestnut for a week." She lifted her cup in a toast. "And you had a good morning."

Clara tried not to blush. The Nightingale would not blush.

Selene laughed. "Good for you, Lady Clara."

She cleared her throat. "Thank you for helping us."

"I thoroughly enjoyed it. I seldom get to balance the scales, you know. I have to be beautiful and charming and sensual. I never get to show my teeth."

As a woman who had to maintain the opposite, Clara commiserated deeply.

And the idea formed in her head almost immediately.

Priya had her network of spinsters and housemaids. Emmeline knew practically every governess in the country. Matilda was friends with most of the bored, wealthy daughters of bored, wealthy men.

"Would you work with us again?" Clara asked. "I could be your liaison with the Society. You would be well compensated, of course."

"I am not exactly a spinster."

"We send out spinsters because they are overlooked, but we have other avenues."

Selene smiled, a genuine smile that showed her slightly crooked eyetooth and the lines at the corners of her mouth. "I would love that."

"I'm so glad. May I visit you at your…house?"

"The brothel. You can say it."

"Very well, the *brothel*." Despite the stories Clara wrote, she had been taught by both her family and Society at large to never say such words aloud or even admit their existence. No brothels or molly houses or mistresses. But Selene had more honor and kindness than most of the *ton*.

"Certainly. We have a private entrance, of course, but also one saved especially for women."

"You do?"

"Yes. I plan to expand." Selene winked. "I look forward to taking your money."

"Excellent. I look forward to a tour."

"So wicked, Lady Clara. It's what I like best about you."

Clara grinned. "I'll be in touch. Excuse me, I have a matter to deal with."

"I'd rather deal with your matter upstairs."

"So would I," Clara muttered. Selene's bright laughter followed her out of the dower house. She crossed the lawn, and the late morning light was incongruously lovely on a house that looked like it was made of cake and sugar frosting but had harbored such darkness.

The house party and Devil's Night were being dismantled, endless trays of glassware being carted down to the scullery for washing. Maids swept; footmen carried furniture back where it belonged. Proper footmen. The marquis's thugs were nowhere to be seen.

Kitty was in her corner, packing up the last of her books into trunks. When she looked up and spotted Clara, she froze.

And promptly burst into tears.

"I'm so sorry," she said, before Clara could even open her mouth on an accusation. She clutched the books in her hands so tightly her knuckles were white.

"You were the blackmailer," Clara said quietly. Her stomach sank at the confirmation.

Kitty nodded miserably, her freckles stark against her pale skin. "I'm sorry," she said again.

"I won't pay you."

"I know. I wouldn't pay me either."

"Why would you do that?"

"I never meant… I panicked. My sister… Well, never mind. It doesn't excuse what I did. Only know I was trying to help my sister."

"By scaring me and threatening me."

"I never threatened you!" Kitty made a face. "Not exactly. And you're never scared of anything."

Clara stared at her. "Are you mad? You sent notes to my house. And here! I was terrified."

"You told me you left directions with your publishers. I invented a bookshop crisis. But I never even went to the fountain," Kitty rushed to add. "You have to believe me. I never would have gone through with it."

"I'm glad to hear it, because I can't think why you would assume I have *five thousand pounds*." The amount was still staggering.

"Your books do so well, and…I just thought… Clara, I don't expect you to forgive me. But I really am so very sorry. More than I can say." Kitty closed the last trunk and stepped aside for a footman to take it to the waiting carriage. "I'll find another bookshop who can be your liaison."

"You won't tell me why you did it?"

"Does it matter? Would it change what I did?"

"I don't know."

Kitty's eyes were bloodshot, and she looked exhausted down to her bones. And scared. "To make a very long and sordid story short, my father gambles." She waved at the detritus of Devil's Night all around them with a sneer. She did not notice Devil at the balcony overhead. "And now my sister is in trouble. I didn't know what to do. I still don't."

It was not an unusual situation. Which did not make it any less awful.

"When you get back to London," Clara said, "talk to the Spinster Society. They'll help your sister."

"Even now?"

"Your sister did not blackmail me. I wish you'd come to us first."

Kitty smiled sadly. "Me too."

CHAPTER THIRTY

CLARA DID NOT have a chance to be alone with Bram before they left for London, nor on the journey back. Sybil sat next to her, itching to get back home and chattering the entire way. Heloise and Martin followed in another carriage, and just as soon as they visited the solicitor, they would be married by special license. Devil had worked whatever nefarious magic he employed to get impossible things done quickly and had the wagers and winnings sorted before sundown.

Rosalinde felt too enclosed in the carriage and opted to join Blanche on her way back to Wales, where they could stop whenever Rosalinde needed to walk the fields and feel the sun on her face.

It boggled the mind that they had only been gone for less than a fortnight. London was the same.

Clara was not.

When they pulled up to the Spinster House, Bram helped them out of the carriage. He paused, bringing his lips to Clara's ear. "I'll see you soon."

And then he climbed back inside and rode away.

Clara did not know what to think about that.

Priya waited on the front step, wearing her usual dirt-stained apron, her gold bangles flashing. Matilda and Emmeline crowded behind her. "Well done, you," she said. "Come and have a cup of tea."

Tea was, naturally, whiskey in the parlor.

Heloise and Martin were shown to a guest room while Sybil sprawled on the settee, kicking her shoes halfway across the room. "I am famished. I can't stop eating. I think I ate an entire wheel of cheese this morning."

Clara sat as well but did not sprawl. Some habits were too ingrained. "I saw it. It was…disconcerting."

"A natural wonder, you mean."

"There was nothing natural about it."

"I also ate a scone," Sybil said in her own defense.

"Four scones," Clara corrected her. "And all of the currant jam."

"I am sure she needs to get her strength back," Matilda offered.

"She does," Clara agreed. "But that jam was my favorite. She nearly bit my hand when I reached for it."

"It's nothing to the name you called me," Sybil said, both proudly and cheerfully. "Our Lady Clara has the mouth of a sailor."

If they only knew.

"Not to mention, she got herself kidnapped to save us and wagered at cards with the marquis right under the Devil's nose." Sybil lifted her glass in a toast. "To Lady Clara, as badly behaved as the rest of us."

Clara smiled demurely.

"Hah," Sybil said. "I don't believe that smile anymore. You can't fool me."

SOON, AS IT turned out, was a very subjective word.

It had been two weeks and Bram had not returned.

The marquis was confined to his townhouse while the House

of Lords and Parliament debated what to do with him. For his multiple murders he was forced to forfeit his title and his estates, and under the *corruption of blood*, his entire lineage would be stricken from the peerage. One of his men managed to sneak him out of London onto a ship bound for France. Rosalinde, not inclined to be forgiving over the murder of her grandfather, sent men after him. Clara did not ask any further questions. As the other five women who had disappeared under the marquis's care or attention over the last decade had not been found, she was also not inclined toward forgiveness.

Meanwhile, Bram sent a message the first night: *Don't forget me.*

The next day, flowers arrived: orchids.

And the day after that.

But no Bram.

Clara finally sent the household away for the night so they would stop shaking their heads sympathetically when she asked if that had been a knock at the door. She needed to work on her next book, to look over the publisher's new contracts.

To obsess over Bram.

Was their time together that morning at the dower house their last time together? She was a dalliance. She'd known that from the start, despite his words to the contrary. She understood the ways of the world for a spinster.

She did not regret a single moment of it.

Not even now, floating aimlessly through her quiet and empty house. She ate bread and cheese for dinner and made a truly terrible cup of coffee. She had thought it would make her feel elegant and confident, like Selene. It might have, had she not had to chew so much of it.

She tried to read, tried to write a new book, now that she was no longer being blackmailed. She still did not quite know how to feel or what to think about Kitty. Part of her wanted a proper row about it. Another part of her could sympathize with running out of options and doing anything to protect your family. Clara did not have that, but she imagined she might be pushed to do the same.

She had hoped that Bram might be her family. That he might stay with her and she with him.

Silly.

Because here she was, back in her townhouse, alone with the candles. The light flickered on the window glass and the carriages rolling by in the wet streets. The rain was falling again, silver tossed over cobbles and roof tiles and lampposts.

And a man, leaning against that lamppost just as he had so many days ago, oblivious to the weather. A sturdy shadow with wide shoulders and thick, curling hair touching the collar of his coat.

Captain Bram Thorn.

He looked up as if she had said his name out loud, as if he had heard her even over the patter of rain and the clatter of carriage wheels and horses' hooves on stone. His eyes burned through her, still and deep and as blue as the sea. Her breath caught in her chest when he pushed out of his lean and stalked down the path to her front door.

She threw it open with very little thought to decorum.

Inviting a man inside her house, at this hour. Marked by scars and tattoos. With that particular intense expression on his face.

"Lady Clara."

"Captain Thorn." Why was he being so polite? Why wasn't he kissing her?

Perhaps he did not want to kiss her. Perhaps this really was goodbye.

Her throat tightened.

"Are you going to invite me in, lass? A man could drown out here."

"Oh." She paused too long, caught herself. "Oh! Do come in. Why were you waiting out in the rain?"

"I assumed you were out. The house was dark." He smelled like rain and sweet limes. Like Bram. The frown he sent down her dark hallway was also pure Bram. "Where's your butler?"

"I don't have one."

"Footman?"

"One and a maid. They'll be back tomorrow."

"You're here alone?" The frown turned to a scowl.

She had to smile. "My footman is barely seventeen years old and weighs less than I do."

"That is not comforting."

"It's Mayfair. Perhaps not Grosvenor Square, but still. I hardly expect an attack." He grumbled under his breath, turning to investigate the lock on her door. "Did you come to assess my defenses, Captain Thorn?"

"Someone has to," he muttered. "And no, of course not."

"Perhaps we could put a cannon on the front step."

"Don't be ridiculous—a moat would be better."

"I'll keep that in mind."

"Clara?"

"Yes?"

"At ease, sailor."

She narrowed her eyes at him but relaxed her shoulders nonetheless. She hadn't realized they were all but tucked under her ears. "If you've come to tell me what we had was temporary, can you do it quickly?"

"Is that why you think I've come?"

"It's been over two weeks," she said. "You disappeared."

"I went to Scotland. I don't know how you all travel by land—it takes twice as long as it should, and there's bloody mud everywhere. I never thought I'd be grateful my sister moved to the Lowlands. If I'd tried to go to Inverness, I'd still be there."

"You never said." He hadn't been in London, at the docks or at the pubs, forgetting about her.

"I said I would be back—" He opened his mouth, closed it. "Damn it. You're right."

"I am?"

"Of course you are. I should have said something more, been

clearer. But goodbyes are bad luck at sea. Though since the carriage threw a wheel anyway and I spent two days in the mud, I should have risked it. I sent a messenger but ended up overtaking him somewhere outside Hammersmith. It was a disaster. Even before my sister threw a glass duck at my head because I did not bring you home with me. I see she was entirely in the right." He did look tired. His boots had definitely spent some time in mud. "I deserved a brick to the head, not just an ornament, if I made you doubt me."

She shrugged one shoulder, but hope was unfurling in her chest again. "You don't owe me anything."

"That's my fault again," he said. "That you would say something so absurd. I swear you'll never have cause to doubt me again. If I'm not with you, Clara, it's only because I'm on my way."

Disbelief, happiness, nerves. Love. It all washed over her at once. For some reason, a giggle bubbled in the back of her throat.

"I went to fetch my grandmother's ring, you see," he added, closing in on her so she had to tilt her head back to meet his gaze. She saw heat, affection, raw need. "But I'm still not part of your world, Clara."

"I'm not really part of my word either."

"I love you. I've loved you longer than I care to admit to."

"You...have?" She clutched his arms because she couldn't bear *not* to be touching him for a moment longer. "How can that be possible? When I've loved you even longer? A war hero and Miss Vinegar."

"What did I tell you about how you talk about yourself?" That stern command that made her shiver deliciously. "You are everything to me. Beautiful and clever and more mischievous than anyone would ever guess. And I happen to like a little vinegar, a little bite to my sweet. So will you marry me, pirate?"

He pulled the ring from his pocket, a simple gold band with a small ruby. A red ribbon fell out.

Her missing red stocking ribbon.

She caught it. "You stole that from me!"

"It's my good-luck charm. Give it back." He plucked it out of her fingers, trading it for the ring. "It's not much, maybe not good enough. Definitely not good enough for you."

The ruby was the same shade as her stocking ribbon. A secret just for her. A ring perfect for Miss Vinegar *and* the Nightingale. "It's perfect."

"We can even live in this cursed city if that's what you want."

"You hate London."

"I love you."

Warmth suffused her. "I don't need to live in London. But I think you need to live somewhere close to the sea."

He touched his forehead to hers. "I only need to live somewhere close to you."

"And the sea," she insisted.

He smiled. "All right, then."

To have a chance to shed some of the constraints she had put on herself, the parts of her disguise that chafed...with Captain Bram Thorn. She could have laughed aloud. Wept. Everything.

"Is that a yes?"

Every part of her screamed yes.

But still she hesitated.

His scarred knuckles lifted her chin. "Talk to me."

"I have a secret."

He smiled fondly. "I have no doubt."

"Do you know the Nightingale?"

"The authoress? Yes."

"She's me," Clara blurted out. "I'm her."

He raised one eyebrow slowly. Was he shocked? Disgusted? She couldn't tell.

"I know," he finally said.

She blinked at him. "What?"

"I already know that."

She shook her head. "What?" she said again.

"I've read everything you've written," he said against her

mouth, closing in on her, pressing her back against the wall. "Twice. I especially like the one with the valet."

"You have?" she asked breathlessly. "You do? How is that possible?"

He kissed her slowly, deeply, until she forgot what they were talking about. "Are you going to marry me or not, pirate?"

She kissed him back. "Of course I am."

The tension softened in his shoulders. She twined her arms around his neck and stretched on her tiptoes to kiss him, to press her entire body against him. He responded by hauling her even closer, urging her legs up so he could carry her. "Where's your bedroom?"

"Top of the stairs and to the left."

His hardness pushed against her, nudging her bud with every step until her breaths became tiny gasps. She was naked by the time her back hit the coverlet, and she wasn't entirely sure how he had managed it. She whimpered when he pulled back enough to divest himself of his own clothing. The swallow tattooed over his heart now held a curling ribbon in its beak. Her silk stocking ribbon.

He lowered himself, hard and hot against her, pressing her into the mattress until there was nothing but him.

Almost.

She wasn't a suitable wife for a captain. She didn't know how to make tea, or tie knots, or do whatever it was captain's wives did. And one day her alternate persona would be revealed. Perhaps she was in no danger from Kitty, but it was probably a matter of time. Secrets had a way of coming out.

He gripped her quim, pressing his palm over her bud. "Pay attention," he commanded. "You're thinking too hard."

"What happens to your career if everyone finds out who I really am?"

"I don't give a damn. I sold my commission months ago. And no one is going to find out who you are if you don't want them to. I'll make sure of it."

"I suppose no one would suspect the Nightingale to be living in a cottage by the sea."

"Captains claim their share of the ships they overtake," Bram told her, running his nose along her throat, inhaling. "And we overtook a bloody lot of ships. I can buy you a grand house."

"I don't need a grand house."

"And I don't need the sea more than I need you. So a grand house by the sea it is." His lips curved against her before he sucked on her lower lip, tugging it gently between his teeth. "I want all of you, Clara. Spinster and pirate and authoress of wicked books." He drew her knees up, nudging her with the tip of his hard cock, dragging it between her folds. "Now, have I got your attention, lass?"

"Y-yes."

His smiled was wicked, hungry. "I don't think I do."

He paused, and she tried to lift her hips up, chasing that friction. He wouldn't let her. His fingers closed gently but firmly around her throat, and it lit something inside of her—his tattooed knuckles against her pale skin, the bold strength of him. "Hold fast," he said, voice gone deep and tender. "Will you let me?"

She nodded, curling her own fingers around his arm. "Don't let go."

He pushed into her heat, and she arched to meet him, gasping.

"Never," he promised.

About the Author

Alyxandra Harvey lives in an old stone house with her husband, multiple dogs, and a few resident ghosts who are allowed to stay as long as they keep company manners. She likes chai lattes, tattoos, and books. Sometimes fueled by literary rage.

Author of The Drake Chronicles, The Witches of London, Haunting Violet, Red, Love Me Love Me Not.

Twitter: AlyxandraH
Instagram: alyxandraharveyauthor